Surrender

Balm in Gilead, Book Two

NOELLE ADAMS

ONE

Vivian Harper scanned her computer monitor, searching for a good image.

When she found a cute photo of a pair of stylish heels in an unusual shade of orange-rose, one sitting upright and the other fallen over on an aged, oak-planked floor, she pulled it up, wrote out two quick sentences, and pinned the picture onto one of her boards.

She was scanning for another good image when a voice came from the doorway of her office. "It's time to go home."

She didn't need to look over to know the slightly dry voice belonged to her business partner, Jeff. "It's not even eight yet."

"It's eight forty-two."

Surprised, she peered down at the time in the corner of her monitor and discovered Jeff was right. She hadn't realized it was so late. "I'm almost done here."

Little red notification alerts at the top of the screen showed that more than a hundred people had already saved her last pin to their boards.

Jeff walked in, looking tired and slightly rumpled with his messy, light brown hair and five-o'clock shadow. He'd taken off his suit jacket early that morning, but he still wore the red-and-gold-striped tie.

He always wore a tie even though she'd told him a million times he could wear anything he wanted. The rest of the staff—including her—wore less formal attire to the office, usually unique and stylish. Today she was wearing red capris, a boatneck top with horizontal black-and-white stripes, with designer heels and a vintage scarf. But Jeff never wore anything but suits and ties—bought, Vivian suspected, at discount outlet stores.

Not that it mattered. He was still adorable with his loosened tie and his sleeves rolled up haphazardly.

"What are you working on?" he asked, moving around her desk so he could see her screen.

"I'm pinning."

"You're on Pinterest! For Pete's sake, Viv, why are you wasting your time?"

"You know that a presence on social media is imp—"

"I know that, but your time is way too valuable for *you* to be doing it. Grace can be doing that. Hell, one of the interns could do all that messing around with pins." He spoke the last words like they were describing a strange and mysterious disease. Then he muttered under his breath, "For Pete's sake."

Vivian tried to keep her expression composed as she kept scanning for images, but her lips wobbled slightly.

"What's so funny?" Jeff demanded, slouching down into the chair next to her desk with a resigned sigh.

"Nothing."

"Tell me."

She darted a quick look over to him. "You do know that you're the only real live person I've ever met who uses the expression 'For Pete's sake,' don't you?"

Jeff frowned at her.

She snickered. "Mel and I were talking about it this afternoon."

"It's a normal expression, isn't it?"

"If you're a friend of Beaver Cleaver maybe."

Jeff maintained his frown, although his brown eyes were glinting with a matching amusement. "My mom used to say it."

"I'm sure she did. It's just one more irresistible feature of the Jeff Owen package."

Jeff rolled his eyes at her. "But seriously, you can't be wasting your time on social media. You're already in the office fourteen hours a day. You need to delegate."

Vivian quickly wrote out a couple of sentences and pinned one more image to a board before she lowered her hands and leaned back in her chair, turning more fully toward Jeff. "I know. I'd like to. But Grace doesn't do the pins right."

"I've seen what she does. They look fine."

"Most of the images she picks are okay, but what she writes about them is not. Faith and Fabulousness is supposed to be about a Christian approach to culture. I don't want our Pinterest boards to turn into covet factories."

Jeff's lips parted as he thought that through.

"It's a fine line, but we have to hold it," Vivian continued, "or we might as well close down the whole enterprise."

"Okay. Okay. I get that. But the answer isn't for you to do everything. The answer is for you to train Grace so she can do it better."

"I know. As soon as I get some time, I plan on doing that."

"Then it will never get done. You'll never have extra time. You need to make time for it now so you don't have to do everything forever."

"Yeah."

His eyes were serious now as they held hers. "Don't tell me *yeah* like that. Tell me you'll do it."

She experienced a little inkling of resistance—as she always did when it felt like he was trying to control her—but she pushed it aside.

Jeff was her partner—they were sixty-forty partners in Faith and Fabulousness, with her holding the controlling interest. He wasn't an employee. He was allowed to have a say in the company and give her his opinion even when it was different than hers.

Plus she knew he was right.

"Okay. I'll work with her on it. After the retreat."

Jeff nodded. Since their company retreat was in two more days, he could hardly argue that she needed to do it before.

Instead of leaving as she thought would be reasonable, he reached over and dragged her cute wicker inbox over toward him on the desk. Then, without asking, he started culling through the stack of papers.

She sat and watched him, thinking he was both annoying and incredibly attractive despite his fuddy-duddy fashion sense.

A flicker of curiosity crossed her mind about when he would start dating again. His wife had walked out on him more than two years ago, and the divorce had been finalized a year ago.

Despite his stubbornness and occasional bossiness, he was a sweet, old-fashioned guy. Surely he would want to get married again.

She couldn't help but wonder what kind of woman he would choose.

She was tempted to ask, but she didn't. She had a feeling he wouldn't appreciate her intruding on his personal life.

They were close because they were partners, but even back in college—where they'd met—they'd never been intimate friends. It was more like their life paths fell in line with each other perfectly, traveling in exactly the same direction.

"Okay," he said, starting to organize the papers in her inbox into three stacks on her desk. "Some of these shouldn't be on your plate at all. Who gave you all these book proposals?"

"I asked Garrett for them. I wanted to see what's come in."

"Well, Garrett should have narrowed them down a lot more before he passed them on to you. It's ridiculous for you to look at some of this garbage." He shook his head. "*The Gospel According to Gardening*." He started to drop the clipped papers into the recycling bin.

Vivian leaned over to reach for them before they could fall into the bin. "That could be an interesting concept."

"There's nothing interesting about that proposal."

After skimming the top sheet, she sighed and released it back into recycling.

"Garrett needs to narrow it down to a few of the best. I'll talk to him." Jeff had been working while she was looking at the proposal, and he'd now organized her entire inbox. "Okay, these are the only things you should do tomorrow." He patted one of the stacks. "Then this stuff can wait until you get back from the retreat. And this other stuff shouldn't be on your desk at all."

She tried to take the last pile from his lap, but he held it out of her reach.

"No," he said. "Someone else can do this stuff."

"But I like to—"

"I don't care what you like to do. This company can't run without you. What would happen to all our jobs if you have a nervous breakdown from stress and lack of sleep?"

She made a face to show she wasn't happy, but she didn't object any further.

Thirteen years ago, during her first year of college, she'd started a blog so she could ramble on about her thoughts about fashion, travel, food, books, and decorating from a Christian perspective. Slowly she'd gained a following, and the blog had become more and more popular. Seven years ago, she'd teamed up with Jeff, who'd been talking to her about the blog's potential since college, and they'd turned the blog into a profitable company. It was far more than a blog now. They had an online store, published a line of books, and put their name and brand behind a wide variety of cultural products.

She'd still just be doing a blog if it hadn't been for Jeff. She knew culture, and she had a lot she wanted to say about how Christians could be "in the world" but not "of it." But Jeff was the one who understood business and made the whole enterprise run.

They now had a staff of six full-time employees and a revolving set of four or five interns. They had a stylish office suite in Raleigh, and she was making more money than she'd ever dreamed was possible with her particular skill set.

None of it would have happened without Jeff.

He was standing up, holding the stack of papers he'd stolen from her inbox against his chest. "You know, if you'd relent and do all your work online like the rest of us, I could organize everything for you before it ever got to you."

She shook her head. "I like to read on paper. I like images online and words on paper."

"Luddite."

She narrowed her eyes at him. "And just think about where the recycled paper industry would be without me."

"Out of business," he said with a chuckle, leaving her office. "Don't work too late."

"Same to you."

Jeff always chided her for working too late, but he almost never went home before she did.

~

A half hour later, Vivian finished answering the most pressing emails in her inbox and was about to turn off her computer when she got a Skype alert.

When she saw it was her parents, she took a moment to check her face, making sure she looked decent. Then she put on a cheerful smile and pulled up the call.

"Hi there!" she said when she saw both of them in the video image reflected back at her. "How are you?"

"We're doing just fine. We're in Belize right now," her mother said.

"I thought you were in Mexico City."

"We just flew down from there today. We're going to be working with a church here for the next two weeks. They've set up a temporary medical clinic and need some help with it. We just heard about the opportunity, so we came right away."

Vivian's parents had retired from full-time ministry five years ago, but they were anything but retired. They spent at least half their time on short-term mission trips and service projects all over the world.

"Is it the same church in Belize you worked with two years ago?"

"Yes. In the same village. The pastor called us and told us about the clinic and some of the needs they have, so here we are." Her mother always did the talking on their Skype calls. Her father was a man of few words, but he always smiled and nodded after everything her mother said, so she knew he was participating in the conversation.

"That's great," Vivian said. "I'm glad you were able to get down there."

"How are things with you, Vivian?" her mother asked.

"They're good. Really good." Vivian felt a little flutter in her chest as she added, "Our latest book—the one on shoes—has been on the *USA Today* best-seller list for two weeks."

She saw her mother glance over to her father with a particular expression. Then she said, "That's wonderful, dear. I guess a lot of people like that kind of thing. *Shoes.*"

Vivian felt a familiar sinking feeling at the implication of that remark. "It's really not as trivial as it sounds," she replied, holding on to her smile. "The book is really on the gospel in culture."

"Of course it isn't trivial, dear. I'm glad you're able to entertain people with that."

Her father nodded his agreement.

Then her mother added, "Did you hear about your sister's latest community service project with the kids at her school?"

The lump in Vivian's throat was old, familiar. From the beginning, her parents had always believed all she did was "entertain" people in a trivial, superficial way. Her sister was the principal at an inner-city mission school in Milwaukee, and her brother was a doctor working with poor villages in the north of India.

And Vivian blogged about shoes and gardens and the recent trends in fiction.

She didn't come out of that comparison looking good.

She finished the conversation, trying to push down the feelings of not being good enough. As they were wrapping up, her parents both told her they loved her and were praying for her.

"I love you too," she said with one last smile. "I'm praying for you too."

Then they said goodbye. Vivian closed down Skype and then shut off her computer.

Then she sat staring at the blank screen for a minute.

She wasn't sure how long she'd been sitting when a familiar voice came from her doorway. "Time to go home."

She turned her head and blinked at Jeff. "Yeah. Right."

Jeff came over, turned her chair to face him, and then grabbed her upper arms to lift her up. He was a few inches taller than her, but her heels made up some of the difference. "Time to go home," he said again.

She let out her breath and smiled at him. "I was just leaving." She got her red purse out of the bottom drawer of her desk and turned off the antique lamp on her desk.

"I'll walk you home," Jeff said.

"You don't have—"

"I need the exercise anyway. I've been at my desk all day."

Vivian lived in an expensive apartment, about half a mile from their office suite. Jeff had a house in one of the Raleigh suburbs, so he always drove to work.

They walked down three flights of stairs and out onto the sidewalk without speaking, and then they turned in the direction of her apartment.

"I heard you talking to your parents," Jeff said, sounding casual, idle, like he was just making conversation.

"Oh. Yeah. I guess I had the volume too loud. Sorry."

"Didn't bother me. How are they doing?"

"Fine. They're in Belize now. Working with some sort of health clinic with a local church."

"They do a lot of that kind of thing, I guess."

"All the time." She felt exhausted and strangely depressed, which wasn't really like her. She was normally an upbeat, optimistic person. Everyone said so.

"Do you always put on your game face before you talk to them?"

She stared at him in surprise. "What?"

Despite her question, she knew immediately what he was talking about. She always prepared her expression before she talked to her parents—the same expression she prepared before she met with potential investors or fans of the blog.

Her game face.

It was a good way to put it.

"You know what I mean," Jeff said, speaking lightly, casually, as if he were just sharing a passing thought. He was by nature a serious, intentional man, so whenever he used this tone, she knew he was doing it on purpose. "Your game face. Your things-are-all-good-and-I've-got-everything-under-control face."

She gave him a little scowl. "How do you know what my expression was like? You weren't in the room."

"I could hear it in your voice."

"You make it sound bad. It's my normal expression."

"It's not bad," he said, slanting a quick look at her, as if checking to see what she was feeling. "It's just not... completely real."

"Why shouldn't it be real?"

"The way you look right now is real."

"What's your point? You're my partner." She reached over to take his arm companionably. "I don't have to try to impress you."

"Why do you have to try to impress your parents?"

She didn't answer the question, and she let Jeff's arm slip out of her hand.

"They've got to be proud of you," Jeff added.

When she looked over, she saw that his eyes were on her face, even as they walked. She gave a little shrug.

"They must see everything you've accomplished."

"Sure." She tried to smile but didn't really succeed.

"What we're doing is really worthwhile. So many Christians have no idea how to interact with culture—engage it in a way that's thoughtful and productive and meaningful. They really have no idea how to do it. Instead, they put up artificial walls or else absorb everything without ever thinking it through. We don't have to run health clinics or schools to do God's work in the world."

She nodded. "I know that."

They walked in silence for a minute.

Then finally Vivian added, "I just don't know that my *parents* know it."

They'd reached her apartment building, and Jeff pulled to a stop. He turned her around so she was facing him. His hands remained on her shoulders, even after he'd repositioned her body. She gazed up at him, her heart starting to beat strangely, wildly.

When he didn't say anything, she swallowed hard. "What?" she asked hoarsely.

He opened his mouth like he would say something, but then he must have changed his mind.

"What?" she demanded.

"I think your parents will see everything you've done," he said at last, after something like reluctance twisted on his face. "But even if they don't, it doesn't devalue your work in the world."

"I know."

"Do you?"

She nodded because she knew that was the right answer. She had no idea why she felt so trembly and emotional.

It was strange and unsettling and almost embarrassing.

They stared at each other for another minute, and for just a moment she was convinced that Jeff was going to slide his hands up into her hair, lean in toward her, maybe even kiss her.

She was actually holding her breath for it.

She wanted him to.

Wanted it desperately.

Then he gave his head a little shake and took a step back. "All right. Good night."

"Good night. Thanks for walking back with me."

"Anytime."

He waited until she'd gotten inside before he started back down to the parking garage he used.

Vivian took a few deep breaths and pulled herself together.

She must be tired. And maybe kind of emotional after her talk with her parents.

She'd never responded to Jeff this way before.

She relied on him for everything. She certainly wasn't going to be foolish enough to let a few stray feelings get in the way of the good of her company.

She'd turned thirty last year. She was single. She had no children. She hadn't committed her life to the kind of service her family believed in.

Her work was the only thing she had to show for her life in this world.

~

Two days later, she and Jeff were in his old Mercedes on their way down the Outer Banks of North Carolina toward The Balm in Gilead Center for Rest.

Jeff had been the one who had heard about this place—a spiritual and physical rest and retreat center—and he'd been the one to convince her to come visit it as a possible location for a company retreat. He'd been the one to insist that the retreat last an entire week instead of the three days she'd suggested.

Because it had been his idea—and because she had no time to tackle it herself—she'd given the retreat to him to plan and organize after she'd signed off on the concept.

Now she was regretting the decision. Jeff was being very quiet about what he had planned for the week.

"So what's the agenda?" she asked at last. They were only twenty minutes from their destination now, and he hadn't mentioned anything about the schedule, so she had no choice but to ask directly.

He glanced over at her briefly before turning back to the road. "Agenda?"

"Yes. The agenda. You're the one who's planning this thing. Am I allowed to know the agenda?"

"Sure. It's just that there's no real agenda." He wasn't looking at her, and his voice was light and casual.

She found both things very suspicious, very unlike Jeff. "What do you mean there's no agenda. You were supposed to plan the retreat."

"I have. But it's a real retreat. It's not a weeklong business meeting in a nice location, which is what a lot of companies call retreats. We're here to rest and refresh ourselves. We're not here to get things done."

"Okay. I get that, and I'm okay with it—although I think it would be fine if we do some brainstorming and future planning while we're here."

"Maybe we will. But I'm not planning it in as a thing to get done."

His chin was sticking out in that stubborn way he had. Vivian sighed. "Okay. Fine. But we're still going to have to do something to fill up our days. What exactly are we going to be doing for a whole week?"

"The rules of the center require anyone who stays there to do a certain number of physical activities a week and a certain number of creative activities a week. So we'll do things like swim, play tennis, paint, or whatever. They have all kinds of options."

"Okay. That will take us about three hours a day. What are we going to do with the rest of our time?"

"Hang out. Read. Rest. Relax. Lay on the beach."

She rolled her eyes. "So basically we're paying for the whole staff to have a weeklong vacation."

"Exactly." Jeff gave her a quick little smile. "We get the vacation too though. You haven't had one in four years."

"I was in Paris just a few months ago."

"But you were doing stuff for Faith and Fabulousness the whole time. You haven't really taken time off in years."

"And what about you? You haven't had a vacation in…" She thought back. "Almost three years."

The last vacation he'd taken had been with his wife. They'd gone to the Cayman Islands.

He hadn't taken a vacation since, although she was sure he'd really needed one after the divorce.

"I need the rest too," he said.

She studied his face, his intentionally casual expression. Then she sucked in a breath. "Did you plan this whole thing just to get me to take some time off?"

A quick flicker of his brown eyes proved that she was at least partly correct in her suspicion. But he said dryly, "Don't overestimate your own importance. As if I would spend all this time and money just to get you to relax."

She shook her head, feeling strangely fluttery for no good reason.

She worked a lot. She knew she did. And the nature of their work led to a good deal of stress. But she also loved what she did and didn't want to be doing anything else. She wasn't on the verge of a breakdown or anything.

She didn't need an intervention or a forced vacation.

It felt strange to her that Jeff would have gone to such an effort for her. It made her feel very... fluttery.

"What?" Jeff demanded, shooting her looks of close scrutiny.

She shook away the flutters and made a face at him. "I'll play along," she said. "I'll be part of his retreat. All of us have been kind of stressed lately, so I suppose it will be good for us. But I'm not any more stressed than anyone else."

"I never said you were."

"And I don't need a rest any more than you and the others do."

"I never said you did."

"And I'm not cutting the budget of any of my projects just to pay for this. The money has to come out of your budget."

"I've already planned for that."

She wrinkled her nose at him. "You're going to have to rest and relax this week too, you know."

"I know."

"You're not any better at it than I am."

"I know that too."

She frowned. "Why are you being so agreeable all of a sudden?"

He gave her an adorable smile. "Maybe I'm already getting into the relaxation mood. I'm going to be completely laid-back this week."

She couldn't help but laugh.

Jeff was a lot of things—and most of them good—but he wasn't any more laid-back than she was.

~

Vivian had met Cecily Evans, the director of Balm in Gilead, on the two times when she and Jeff had come to check out the place before they'd made the decision to use it for their retreat. Cecily was a few years older than Vivian and was very attractive with ash-blond hair, a slim figure, and a prim, old-fashioned style that Vivian really liked.

Not that Vivian could pull off the style herself, but she liked it on the other woman.

Cecily greeted them when they arrived, wearing a pretty, pink blouse and pencil skirt, and she gave them each a folder with information on the center. Grace and Mel were already here, and the rest of the staff would be coming later.

The building had formerly been a luxury hotel, and it was still in excellent condition, decorated with an elegant beachy style with a lovely tile floor and tasteful art on the wall. Vivian's room was on the third floor, right next to Jeff's. It was large and airy and recently refurnished. It had a large balcony with sweeping views out onto the ocean.

Vivian was impressed.

"Thank you," she said to the man who had carried her luggage up. His name was Zeke, and he was a strange, gruff man with an untrimmed dark beard and the worst taste in clothes she'd ever seen.

Today he wore a pair of orange shorts and a blue T-shirt that didn't match at all.

He grunted, which was more of an answer than she'd ever gotten from him before.

Jeff had taken his stuff to his own room, but now he walked into hers. "What do you think?" he asked.

"It's great," she told him with a smile. "That view is amazing."

Zeke was standing nearby with a silent scowl.

She shot him a few looks, wondering why he wasn't leaving. She already knew that tips weren't allowed at the center, so he couldn't be waiting for that.

Jeff arched his eyebrows. "Phones."

She groaned softly and slumped a little. One of the rules of the center, she already knew, was no laptop, phones, or electronic devices that connected to the internet were allowed. It was one of the ways to ensure a complete break.

From the beginning, Vivian had believed the policy was ridiculous.

"I think it's a bad idea," she said, holding her phone protectively.

"I don't care what you think. You knew the drill coming here. You might have left your laptop at home, but that's not enough. You have to give up your phone too." Jeff had that stubborn look again.

"What if I don't use it? I'll just keep it for emergencies?"

"Hannah and Derek are covering the office," Jeff said, shaking his head. "They'll take care of any emergencies. You said you'd play along." He held out a hand, palm up. "So hand it over."

She groaned again but gave him her phone. Jeff immediately stepped over to Zeke and handed him both Vivian's phone and Jeff's own phone.

Vivian gave him a little sneer.

"It will be good for you to be disconnected for a little while," Jeff said.

Vivian rolled her eyes at him. "Who's the boss around here anyway?"

Jeff met her eyes. "You're not the boss of me."

For some reason the texture in his voice gave Vivian little shivers up and down her spine. She was hit with a wave of attraction that came out of nowhere and was completely inappropriate.

She liked Jeff. More than almost anyone. And she thought he was very cute in his own way.

But he wasn't her type of guy. She usually went for stylish, successful men, most of whom eventually proved to be assholes. Plus Jeff was her business partner, which meant he was completely off-limits for her.

She couldn't be indulging these waves of attraction for him.

She really needed to get them under control.

"You okay?" Jeff asked softly, although Zeke and his scowl had already left the room.

"Yes," she said, just slightly breathless. "Of course. I just didn't want to give up my phone."

His forehead was wrinkled, as if he didn't believe her, but he didn't push the subject. "I'll stop by in an hour so we can go down to dinner together," he said.

She nodded, giving him a bright smile. Her game face. "Sounds good."

Jeff still looked a little confused, a little suspicious, but thankfully he left the room.

She waited until the door had closed with a click. Then she put her purse on the table near the window.

She'd known what she would have to do when she came to this place. She'd known she would have to give up her phone.

But she was good at planning, and she wasn't good at going along with things that didn't make sense to her.

She opened a small zipper pocket of her purse and pulled out another smartphone.

She wasn't going to go a week without a phone. She would just have to keep it secret and only take it out when no one else was around.

If there was anything she did well, it was make things happen the way she wanted them.

Jeff really should have known better.

TWO

The next morning, Jeff knocked on Vivian's door, wondering if there was any way she was really going to rest and relax this week.

He knew her pretty well, and he assumed the most likely scenario would be her making a kind of game of it and then taking a lot of pictures, creating a pretty narrative about the week, and writing an article for Faith and Fabulousness about the necessity of rest and relaxation.

All without ever resting and relaxing herself.

She opened the door to him with a cheerful smile, looking very pretty and perfectly put together in a casual blue dress and stylish sandals. "Morning," she said brightly.

Jeff sighed. The bright, confident, slightly flirtatious manner was typical for her. Her game face, he called it. She wore it like armor—and had since college, when he'd first concluded she was beautiful, brilliant, and untouchable. He knew now that it hid the vulnerability at the heart of her, and sometimes he found it frustrating that she would still try to put on a show for him when she was feeling uncertain about things.

They knew each other too well for that.

She must know that she wasn't fooling him.

He wished she would be more herself—at least in front of him. He wished she would trust him that much.

"Are you grumpy this morning?" she asked, her smile fading slightly at his prolonged silence.

He shook away the futile thoughts. "Of course not."

"Then why are you giving me that disapproving look?"

"I didn't mean to."

"So you were trying to keep your disapproving thoughts about me to yourself?"

He couldn't help but smile at her clever tone. "Of course not. Why would I disapprove of you?"

"I don't know." She was looking more like herself now as they walked down the hall together. "But I know your disapproving look when I see it."

"You're imagining things."

She didn't answer, but her blue-gray eyes made it clear that she knew better.

When they reached the lobby, Vivian stepped out of the elevator and nearly collided with Zeke, who was wearing an ugly, striped shirt and his typical scowl.

"Haven't you heard of saying excuse me?" she asked, smiling and fluttering her eyelashes at Zeke.

Zeke made a wordless grumble and stepped into the elevator.

Vivian laughed softly.

"You shouldn't tease the poor guy," Jeff said.

"Tease him? I don't think that guy would know teasing if it hit him over the head."

"Well, you shouldn't flirt with him or whatever you were just doing."

"I wasn't flirting with him," she said with a frown, taking his arm as they headed into the dining room. "I've just decided my mission over the next week is to get that guy to smile."

"Why bother?"

"Because it's a challenge. What else do I have to do this week?"

"You can focus on taking it easy and hanging out with the rest of us."

She sighed. "You are grumpy this morning. I thought you were going to be Mr. Laid-back this week."

Jeff wasn't by nature a laid-back guy. He worked hard and tried his best and took serious things seriously. Kaylee, his ex-wife, used to say he was a stick-in-the-mud and complain that he didn't know how to let loose.

He couldn't help but wonder if Vivian thought the same of him.

"I am," he said. "Mr. Laid-back. That's me for the week."

Vivian just laughed.

~

Jeff and Vivian's staff consisted of six full-time employees. Grace, smart and perky and in her midtwenties, who was Vivian's assistant. Melody, always known to the office as Mel, who was in her fifties and handled most of the marketing. Rachel O'Brien, who was an interior decorator by training and a fashion junkie by preference—and her husband, Garrett, who had a degree in professional writing and managed their line of books. Plus Hal, their IT guy, and Vince, Jeff's assistant.

The O'Briens were the newest addition to the staff, and they'd been working for Faith and Fabulousness for almost two years. So they all knew each other really well. The staff was really as much like a family as a company, and Jeff knew that Vivian wanted it that way.

They usually got along quite well, although the occasional spat was inevitable. Vivian usually left it to Jeff to make sure everyone was behaving themselves and doing their job, because she hated conflict and confrontation.

Vivian was the inspiration, the idea person, the heart and voice behind the company.

Jeff just made sure things got done.

So it wasn't a surprise when, after they'd finished eating breakfast and had fallen into silence, Vivian looked over at Jeff. Her eyebrows lifted. "So should we do something?"

Jeff already knew what he was going to suggest. "We have to do some sort of physical activity today. Rules of the center. Maybe we should do it first, before it gets too hot. They've got a good beach volleyball court."

"Excellent," Garrett said. He was smart and outgoing and had a hipster look with dark-rimmed glasses and hair that always needed cutting. "Rachel is great at volleyball. I'll be on her team. Let's get going now before someone else claims the net."

"Some of us need to change clothes or shoes," Jeff put in. "Let's meet down there in twenty."

The rest of the staff agreed with this plan, but as they were getting up, Jeff lingered because Vivian's expression looked strange.

"What's wrong?" he asked, putting a hand on her arm to stop her from following the others.

She gave him her (fake) bright smile. "Nothing."

He rolled his eyes. "Haven't we talked about you lying to me? Your game face doesn't convince me, you know."

She sighed and thankfully lost that artificial expression. "I don't know how to play volleyball."

He gaped at her. He couldn't help it. "What? You're kidding."

"No, I'm not kidding." She'd narrowed her eyes at him now. "I don't know how to play. I never have before."

"Didn't you play in school? At church picnics? In summer camp?"

"No, I didn't. My family never did that kind of thing."

"What kind of thing did they do?" He'd leveled off his tone now because he could see she was getting defensive.

"We did… community service projects, worked in food banks, went on short-term mission trips. You know what my folks are like, right? You think they'd spend time with something as useless as volleyball when they could be saving the world?"

Her tone was light, but Jeff felt a little twinge in his chest. The same one he'd felt when he'd overhead her discussion on Skype with her parents the other night. He knew she loved her family and they obviously loved her back. He shouldn't judge someone else's priorities or lifestyle. If constant do-good-ery made them happy, then all the better for them.

But he didn't like that Vivian always had to compare herself to those standards; ones that made her feel like she was always falling short.

Any parents, any family, any husband should have been incredibly proud of what she'd done with her life, of the person Vivian was.

Her expression had changed as she'd waited for him to respond. "Jeff?"

He blinked. "Yeah."

"I thought we were having a discussion."

They had been until he'd found himself thinking very inappropriate and futile thoughts about her. "Sorry. I must be tired or something. But don't worry about not playing volleyball before. We're just going to be having fun."

"But I seriously don't know how to play."

"Basically, the idea is to get the ball over the net."

She rolled her eyes at him. "I can just watch."

"No, you can't. You're playing with the rest of us."

"But—"

"But nothing. You're playing."

"You know I don't like it when you're bossy like this, right?" Her blue eyes were flashing at him, and her cheeks were slightly flushed.

For just a moment Jeff had to fight the urge to pull her into a kiss.

He cleared his throat. "I'm sorry you don't like it, but there's no question about this. It's a company retreat. *Your* company. You have to play."

She stared at him for a moment, then nodded. "Okay. Fine."

"You can be on a team with me. I'll help you out."

"Okay."

"It's really not that hard."

"I said okay."

"I'm just saying. You'll probably enjoy it. There are just a couple of things to learn—how to hold your hands and such. You'll pick it up quickly."

"Jeff?"

"What?"

"Has anyone ever told you that you don't know how to take yes for an answer?"

He felt a flicker of amusement and then another flicker of attraction. He was used to the attraction—it was impossible not to find Vivian beautiful, sexy, desirable, smart, generous, brave, funny, everything he might want in a woman—so he focused on the amusement. "Just making sure you're not going to back out," he told her with a twitch of his lips.

She smiled at him, and he felt his heart do a ridiculous gallop. Not just a little trot, which would have been familiar and manageable, but a full-fledged, no-holds-barred, run-for-the-roses gallop.

This wasn't good at all.

"And this is your company too," Vivian added in a different tone.

"What?" He had absolutely no idea what she was talking about because he was consumed with getting his foolish heart back under control.

"You said it was *my* company. It's your company too. It's *ours*. It's always been ours. It wouldn't be anything without you."

And that did nothing to help the state of his heart. He swallowed hard. "Oh. Right."

~

In a little more than twenty minutes, the staff had gathered at the beach volleyball court. Jeff had asked Zeke for a ball, which the other man had provided in typical unsmiling silence.

They divided into two teams, and Jeff made sure he was paired with Vivian. Garrett and Rachel were also on their team, and they both clearly knew what they were doing. Between the three of them, they could cover for Vivian.

As it turned out, they had to. Rachel was a spiker, and Garrett and Jeff were pretty good at setting her up. But Vivian mostly just got out of the way of the ball. Even when it came right to her, she would look over at Jeff, expecting him to get it for her.

After about twenty minutes, he stopped running over to cover for her.

When the other team got three points in a row, Vivian strode over to Jeff, took him by the arm, and said in an annoyed whisper, "You're supposed to be helping me."

"I will help you. But you have to actually play for me to help."

"We were doing fine with you covering for me."

"I don't care. You still have to play." He spoke in the voice he always labeled in his mind his "determined voice." It was low and even and almost laid-back, which was a shift from his normal tone.

"Don't give me your stubborn voice," Vivian said with a scowl.

"Determined voice," he corrected. It was like she had read his mind.

"Stubborn. And it's not going to work this time. I don't know how to play."

"You haven't even tried."

"I don't like doing things I don't know how to do well."

There was the slightest note of vulnerability in her voice, and it struck Jeff hard. He realized she was telling the truth. The absolute truth.

Vivian was good at things—good at almost everything. She was outgoing and confident and used to being in control of her world.

She wasn't used to learning how to do something she didn't already know how to do.

"I know you don't," he murmured, "but I'm not going to cover for you anymore. So you either step up or face the ridicule of the staff for not even trying."

She narrowed her eyes at him, but he could see she wasn't really angry. She was embarrassed and kind of nervous, and the human side of her was just as appealing as the side she showed the rest of the world.

More appealing because she showed it to him but almost no one else.

"Fine," she muttered, returning to her place.

The others had used the break to grab a drink of water and catch their breaths, but they were at it again soon enough.

Vivian did try after that. She missed several times as she worked out how to position her hands, but she eventually picked it up. The ball didn't always go exactly where she was aiming at, but she did pretty well for her first time. She was fit and coordinated. She wasn't going to be terrible at his.

He could see her gaining confidence with each volley, and soon she was obviously comfortable enough to actually be competitive, which was her normal attitude with any game.

They'd played for almost an hour, and Jeff was finally able to focus on the game and not on making sure Vivian was doing all right. Everyone was clearly having fun with a lot of cheerful taunting and rivalry, and Vivian was now joining in.

He was relaxed and enjoying himself, and when the ball came into his quadrant, he did the normal thing and ran over to set up Rachel for a spike.

The ball was kind of in between him and Vivian but definitely more on his side than hers. He certainly didn't expect her to run for the ball too.

They ended up crashing into each other, and the other team got the point.

While the others either cheered or groaned, depending on which team they were on, Jeff tried to pull himself up.

It wasn't as easy as it sounded since he was on the sand in a tangle with Vivian.

He was actually on top of her, and she was warm and soft and feminine and curvy beneath him. His body started thinking things—and doing things—that it definitely shouldn't be thinking or doing.

"I had it!" Vivian complained. She didn't appear to be hurt, and she didn't appear to be perturbed that he was lying on top of her.

"It was on my side."

"But I could have gotten it."

"We're supposed to be on the same team. We take turns."

She scowled at him, and the expression did nothing to distract him from the stirring in his groin, the buzzing in his head, the thudding of his heart. "I was just getting good."

She was good.

She was good at almost everything.

She would probably be good in bed too—passionate and vulnerable both.

He gulped and jerked his body away from hers before his condition became too advanced and potentially noticeable. He breathed heavily and willed his body back into a safer state.

Vivian was looking at him as she stood up, tousled and flushed and beautiful. "Are you mad?" she asked, peering at him closely.

"No, I'm not mad. Just stay on your side."

He wasn't mad. Not at her anyway.

God help him, he was mostly mad at himself.

~

They did activities together all morning and then had lunch together. Then Jeff figured they'd had enough togetherness for the time being and turned everyone loose to amuse themselves for the afternoon.

At about three, Jeff had gone up to his room to shower since he'd walked on the beach and gotten all sandy.

He was thinking about what he should do when he happened to glance down through his window and saw that Vivian was lying out by the pool.

No reason why he shouldn't go down to the pool himself.

He changed into a suit, grabbed his sunglasses and a book he'd brought with him, and headed down.

Vivian waved at him when he came out but didn't invite him over.

He sat on the opposite side of the pool as her, in case she wanted to be alone.

She was wearing one of those two-piece suits that weren't really bikinis. The top came down close to the bottom. But it was still plenty revealing, and he couldn't help but let his eyes linger on the delectable cleavage revealed above her top and the length of her bare legs stretched out on the chaise.

He'd put on his sunglasses, so he could watch her without it appearing obvious. She looked relaxed, like she might be taking a nap in the sun, but he knew she wasn't.

She was awake.

She was probably plotting out her next plans for Faith and Fabulousness. He knew she did that in her "downtime."

After a while, she got up, picked up her bag, and went to the door off the pool deck that led to a bathroom. She came out in a few minutes, and she looked like even less relaxed than she had before.

He kept watching her.

She had a little notepad with her, and she would occasionally jot something down.

She was definitely planning something. Plotting out a blog post or putting together a new project.

She was supposed to be taking it easy.

In less than an hour, she got up again to go the bathroom with her bag.

And he knew—he *knew*—something wasn't right.

He suddenly realized what it must be.

He'd known she'd relented too easily when she'd given up her phone. She'd made a gesture at resistance, but it hadn't been enough.

Jeff got up and walked over to wait outside the bathroom door.

When she walked out again after a few minutes, she jerked slightly when she saw him waiting for her.

"What?" she asked, putting her bag over her shoulder in a protective gesture.

"Hand it over," he said, stretching out his hand with the palm up.

Her frown this time was real. "What are you talking about?"

"You know exactly what I'm talking about. You've taken your purse to the bathroom twice in an hour. I know what you have in it. Now hand it over."

"You're being ridiculous. It's none of your business why I go to the bathroom. I might have... have female problems."

"You don't have female problems. If you don't give me the phone, I'm going to take it from you. I knew you gave in too easily yesterday."

"I don't have a—"

He reached out to put a hand on her shoulder. "Vivian, give it to me right now. You know the rules. You agreed to the rules. And now you're standing there lying to me. Give it to me."

He saw the struggle on her face as she tried to decide between her own will and her sense of duty. Finally she grimaced, let out a soft groan, and reached into her purse. She opened a zipper pocket and pulled out a small smartphone.

"It's a ridiculous rule."

"I don't care. You agreed to it, so you're going to abide by it this week. I'll give this to Zeke."

She was breathing heavily, and her eyes were flashing. He had a quick picture, a visual of how she would look if he was making love to her, her eyes flashing, her breast rising and falling...

"You're a real asshole sometimes, Jeff," she said. She wasn't whining or being petty. She was telling him exactly what she was thinking—the way she almost always did. "You know that, right?"

"Yes, I know that. And you're kind of spoiled and willful sometimes. We all have our issues."

He'd hoped the lighter tone of his voice would spark her humor, but it didn't.

She didn't smile at him.

She wasn't yet resigned to the fact that he'd made her give up her phone.

She returned to her chaise, but she didn't lie back down. She got her water bottle and her hat, and she left the pool deck.

She was really annoyed with him. It wasn't one of their teasing little spats.

It made his stomach twist uncomfortably.

He didn't want her to be annoyed with him. He wanted her to like him.

He wanted her to more than like him.

But it was just as well.

His thinking was obviously starting to run out of control where she was concerned, so this was a helpful reminder to pull himself together.

She was in his life. She would always be in his life. And he always wanted her there.

But she would never look at him as anything except a business partner, so he couldn't let himself hope for anything else.

He'd already given his heart to a woman who didn't want it once, and it had been the most painful, humiliating experience of his life.

He wasn't going to do it again.

THREE

Vivian didn't sleep well that night.

In fact, she didn't sleep at all.

She felt naked—weak and vulnerable—without her phone. She often had trouble shutting down her mind at night, so she would distract and amuse herself by looking at her phone in bed. She would check her email, the Faith and Fabulousness social media sites, read some news and commentary sites she enjoyed, and occasionally play games if she was really bored and restless. But without her phone she couldn't do any of that, so she had to lie in bed, hour after hour, wondering what was happening in the world and worried that she was missing out on something important.

It wasn't a good feeling.

And she couldn't help but blame Jeff for it.

If he'd just minded his own business, she wouldn't have had to give up her hidden phone. No one would have known the difference, and she'd have been able to make it through the week just fine.

Now the six remaining days stretched out in bleak, empty endlessness.

How had Jeff known about the phone anyway? She'd been careful with it. No one had seen it. It was like he'd read her mind or something.

Another feeling she really didn't like.

She took a long shower and blew her hair dry, working herself back into her game face so she could socialize with the others today. She didn't feel like it. At all. She mostly felt like hibernating, preferably with her phone.

But obviously she didn't have a choice.

She was the boss here, so she had to act like she was having a grand time and didn't want to be anywhere else.

When she heard a knock on her door, she knew it was Jeff. She overcame the urge to just let him keep knocking and opened the door with a smile.

He was dressed in cargo shorts and a green golf shirt, and she was immediately hit with how appealing he was—cute and lean and masculine and serious—just a little uptight. His eyebrows lowered. "Didn't you sleep well?"

Okay, this was getting annoying. She'd put on makeup and dressed in bright pink. She looked fresh and perfectly pulled together. There was no way Jeff should be able to tell that she'd lain awake all night.

"I slept fine," she told him, forcing a smile.

When it looked like he was going to continue the topic, she added, "Let's go on down. I'm starving this morning."

She wasn't starving. She just didn't want to have the conversation Jeff appeared to want to have.

He didn't look convinced—or particularly happy—but he didn't argue as they walked down the hall to the elevator and then descended to the ground floor to head into the dining room.

They were the first of the staff down this morning, so they headed over to the breakfast bar and loaded up their plates with eggs, fruit, biscuits, and sausage gravy.

Vivian didn't usually eat breakfast, and she would prefer to just have toast and coffee this morning. But she'd told Jeff she was starving, and so she was trapped by the lie.

One reason it was usually better to just tell the truth.

She stared down at her full plate and realized she would have to eat it. She felt terrible. She was exhausted. She was starting to get a headache.

And she missed her phone.

"It's like withdrawal, isn't it?" Jeff said, having prayed silently for a few seconds and now starting to dig into his own plate.

"What is?"

"Going without your phone."

She scowled at him.

"Clearly it affects your mood. Like withdrawal." His voice was very dry.

She tried to smooth the scowl from her face. She was over thirty. She didn't want to get wrinkles just because Jeff was being an ass. "You don't have to gloat about it."

"Does it sound like I'm gloating?"

"Yes. It really does."

"Well, I'm not." His voice wasn't dry anymore. It was characteristically serious. His deep brown eyes were scanning her face with an intensity that made her self-conscious. "I meant it. It's like withdrawal."

"Why aren't you having any trouble with it?"

"I don't think I was ever as tied to my phone as you are, but I do find it kind of frustrating not to be able to check in. But I've got other things to think about."

"Like what?"

"Like making sure you're not going off the deep end."

Her attempt at saving her skin from wrinkles failed utterly. She snarled at him. "I'm not going off the deep end. You really think I'm having a breakdown or something?"

"No. Of course not. But you're clearly having a hard time with it."

"Why do you think that?"

"Because you're usually in a better mood than this."

He was right. Of course he was right. After her two cups of coffee in the morning, she was usually cheerful and ready to start the day. It wasn't just an act. She liked what she did, and she enjoyed going to the office. She liked the people she worked with.

Even Jeff.

When he wasn't being an ass.

"Maybe it's not the phone that's the problem," she snapped. "Maybe it's you."

He was about to say something in response, but Garrett and Rachel had arrived a few minutes ago and were heading over to their table with smiles and loaded plates.

Vivian let out a breath and put on a matching smile to greet them, relieved that the discussion with Jeff was over.

It wasn't like he could snipe at her in front of the rest of the staff.

~

They played tennis that morning after breakfast—something Vivian knew how to do and was good at, so she wasn't as uncomfortable as she'd been the day before.

After that, they needed to do a creative activity, required by the rules of Balm in Gilead. No one had any strong ideas about what they should do, but Mel enjoyed scrapbooking and suggested they do that. There was a dedicated room filled with supplies, and it seemed like a harmless enough activity, so they all agreed.

Vivian didn't actually enjoy it, although she joked and laughed with the others as they took and printed out photos of themselves and their surroundings and then put them into a book filled with fancy paper, cutouts, and stickers.

Her pages looked really nice, so she'd obviously done a decent job participating in the activity.

Jeff wasn't any good at it, and she couldn't help but enjoy that fact.

She felt petty and silly whenever she recognized how she was thinking, and she tried to clear her mind of her bad mood and focus on the task at hand. But it felt like she was faking it, putting on a mask, filling a role she was supposed to fill.

It was better than pouting though, and no one seemed the wiser.

They'd been working for more than an hour and were nearly finished with their little book when she got up to go to the bathroom, having drunk too much coffee and then water this morning.

She was on her way back to the room when she was surprised to see Jeff in the hallway waiting for her.

He was frowning at her again.

What the hell did he want now?

"What?" she asked in a soft voice, although they were alone in the hall.

"This is supposed to be a retreat for you too, you know," he said, just as quietly as she had.

"What are you talking about?"

"Can't you let down and be yourself even for a morning?"

She gaped at him. They were usually honest with each other, and they didn't always have perfectly nice things to say to each other, but all he'd done was criticize her for the past two days. She had no idea what had gotten into him.

"I am being myself," she replied coolly.

"No, you're not. You've got your game face on again. You're putting on a show for them." He waved toward the door to the craft room to indicate the rest of the staff. "You're trying to present yourself to the world in a certain way, the way you always do—as if you were one of your rooms to decorate or photos to stage. You're not, and that's not what we're here for. So maybe, for once, you can try to be real for a little while."

She stared at him blindly for a moment as she processed his words.

It felt like he'd hit her or stabbed her in the chest. It literally hurt that bad.

It was one thing for him to criticize her for sneaking in a phone or being crabby that morning—that was understandable, and she'd probably deserved it.

But this was far deeper than that.

This was the person she was.

He thought she was fake. He thought that fake was all she was.

And she'd stupidly believed that Jeff was one of the few people who truly loved her.

She swallowed over the lump in her throat. There was no way she could speak, so she didn't even try. She wasn't the kind of person who walked away when someone said something mean to her. She'd always been someone who fought back.

But this simply hurt too much.

She stepped around Jeff, not really seeing him through the blur in her eyes, and she returned to the room with the others.

They were laughing over a joke that Garrett had made, so Vivian asked what it was. She laughed too when they told her.

Jeff returned to the room shortly after she did, and she could feel him watching her for the ten minutes it took for them to finish their book.

He looked like he had something to say to her, but she didn't want to hear it.

Mostly she wanted to get away and cry for a minute, but she didn't have the leisure, so she smiled and smiled and smiled and smiled and tried not to think about what Jeff evidently thought about her and waited to finally be alone.

~

She got through lunch with the rest of the staff, and they all agreed to again do their own things that afternoon, as they had the day before. As soon as she could make an escape, she hurried up to her room and closed the door, finally feeling safe, like she was shutting out the rest of the world.

She wasn't really near tears anymore, but she felt sick and depressed and so exhausted she could barely move. She kicked off her shoes, pulled the ponytail holder out of her hair, and collapsed on her bed.

She wondered how long Jeff had thought this about her.

She wondered how long he'd been waiting to say something to her about it.

She wondered if she really was just fake, focused only on appearances, not doing or being anything genuine.

Her parents probably believed the same thing about her.

She really needed her phone right now to distract herself, to help push these thoughts out of her mind.

Everyone got hurt and depressed sometimes. She was human like everyone else. But she was usually able to focus on other things and get over them fairly quickly.

But she had absolutely nothing to focus on right now. No phone, no computer, no television, no tablet. She had a book but didn't have the energy to read.

She had nothing but her thoughts.

She hated feeling this way.

She *hated* it.

She'd only been lying on her bed for fifteen minutes when there was a knock on her door.

She knew it was Jeff.

She *knew* it.

And she really didn't want to talk to him.

She waited for about thirty seconds. Then the knock came again.

"Go away," she called out.

"I'm not going away. Let me in." Jeff's voice. Sounding very serious and slightly impatient.

"I'm taking a nap."

"No, you're not. Let me in." He kept knocking.

She waited for another minute, but the knocking continued.

No one was as stubborn as Jeff. He'd stand there knocking for an hour if she didn't open the door, and she just didn't have the energy to deal with that this afternoon.

She groaned softly as she got up and went to the door. She swung the door open and blinked at him. "What?"

"Are you going to let me in?"

"No. I told you I was napping. What do you want?"

"I want to talk to you." He glanced down the hall when someone's voice drifted in their direction. "Do you really want to have this discussion in the hallway?"

She sighed and stepped aside so he could come in.

He must have taken a shower because the edge of his hair was slightly damp. He had on another golf shirt. He nearly always wore shirts with collars.

At least he wasn't wearing a tie today.

He took about four steps into the room and just looked at her as she closed the door.

When he didn't say anything, she arched her eyebrows. "You're the one who wanted to talk."

He opened his mouth and then closed it again without speaking.

"What?" she said. "If you have more criticism of me, then just spit it out."

"I'm so sorry, Vivian," he said in a hoarse rush. "I'm so incredibly sorry for hurting you."

She hadn't been expecting the apology, and it caught her off guard. She was hit with a wave of emotion—one left over from earlier than day and intensified by her lack of sleep.

Jeff took a step closer to her and reached out to take her hand. He held it in both of hers. "I mean it, Viv. I'm so sorry."

"Okay," she managed to say. "It's not that big a deal."

"Yes, it is. I hurt you. I can see how much."

She gave a little shrug. "It's mostly because I didn't get enough sleep last night."

He shook his head, his eyes deep and tender. "No, it's not. I hurt you, and I never wanted to do that."

He was still holding her hand. His were warm and surprisingly strong. The touch made her feel strange—good and excited and jittery.

She gently pulled her hand free. "It's okay," she said, dropping her eyes and then raising them briefly back to his face. "We've always been honest with each other. If you had something to say, then you could say it."

"But it came out wrong. It came out like I was... like I was judging who you are. And I didn't mean it like that."

"Then how did you mean it?"

"I just wanted you to relax a little and be yourself. You don't always have to put on a perfect front for everyone. But it came out all wrong, and I know I hurt you, and I wouldn't do that for the world."

She could see he meant it. He was completely vulnerable. Completely earnest.

It made her feel good and jittery in a different way.

She swallowed and gave a little nod. "Okay. Thanks for saying that."

He stood in front of her without moving for a moment. "So," he began at last. "So we're okay?"

"Of course we're okay. I'm not so petty and immature that I'd hold a grudge. Did you think I would?"

"No, of course not. I just don't want you to still be thinking about it. I don't want you to still be upset."

"I'm not upset."

"You look upset to me. You've been crying."

"No, I haven't." To be safe, she slid her fingertips under her eyes to make sure her mascara hadn't been running. "I told you. I'm tired. I didn't get any sleep last night, and then you woke me up from my nap."

"You weren't napping." For the first time, a little smile played on the corners of his mouth.

It made her want to smile back, but she didn't. "I was about to."

"Okay. I'll let you get back to it then. As long as you're really going to sleep and not just brood about what I said."

"You're overestimating your own importance again. I never brood about what you say." She walked with him toward the door, relieved they were back to their normal interaction. Then she heard herself adding, "But I'm not always trying to put on a show or presenting myself to the world like I'm a photo to be staged."

He paused, his expression changing. "Not all the time, no. But sometimes you do."

"I do not."

She didn't know why she was arguing. She'd almost gotten him out of the room so she could be alone, but now he wasn't going anywhere. He'd come to a dead halt, and his eyes were searching her face in that way he had, the one that made her nervous and self-conscious.

"You know you do sometimes, Viv. Everyone does to a certain extent. It's how we learn to interact with each other. But you do it in a different way, when you think that what you're really feeling or thinking or doing isn't quite up to

45

snuff. I've known you for years, Viv. I know you better than anyone. There's no sense in lying to me about it."

She had that lump in her throat again, but it was different this time. It didn't feel like he was criticizing her. It felt like he was telling the truth, and she wished the truth was otherwise.

Maybe her parents were right about her—that she'd spent her life pursuing superficial entertainment—and it had made her superficial herself.

"I can't help thinking," Jeff was going on, "that you put on the pretty picture because you don't think there's anything real in you to show."

Her lips parted slightly, and she almost swayed on her feet. "Maybe there's not," she heard herself whispering.

He shook his head and reached out to cup her cheek with one hand. "Yes, there is, Viv. You know there is when you're thinking clearly, when these lies aren't clouding your thinking. You *know* there is. And I know there is too."

She let out a breath and realized she was leaning her face into his warm hand. She took a step back and felt shaky, so she walked over to sit down on the edge of her bed.

Jeff came over to sit down beside her.

She gave him a little smile, trying to feel more like herself. "You're getting to be kind of a know-it-all lately."

He gave a soft huff of amusement. "Maybe on this subject, I do know it all."

"What subject?"

"You." His eyes were deep and soft and tender again, and they were doing very disturbing things to her heart. She had to look away.

"Do you know the first time I saw you?" he asked.

"We met at the RUF meeting in college." She remembered it very clearly. She'd gone with her roommate to a weekly meeting of one of the campus ministries in her first semester in college, and she'd sat down next to Jeff. After it was over, he'd introduced himself to her very soberly and even stuck out his hand for her to shake.

She'd thought he was cute and kind of nerdy. No one shook hands back in college.

"That was when we first met. It's not when I first saw you."

"When did you first see me?"

"At one of the freshman orientation events."

"You were two years ahead of me."

"I was working the orientation. And there you were, pretty and blond and smiling and already having other kids swarming around you like you were the most fragrant flower in the garden. I figured you were one of those girls." His mouth twisted slightly. "You know, the popular ones who... who don't have a lot going on underneath."

"Maybe that's who I am."

He shook his head. "Ralph was clearing dishes in the dining hall when we went in for lunch. Do you remember Ralph?"

"Yeah, I think so. The one who stuttered."

"Yes. That's him. Anyway, he was kind of weird-looking, and everyone kind of gave him a wide berth. And when you walked by, he stared at you and got distracted and dropped his tray of dishes. You went over and helped him pick them up."

Vivian was trying to remember the incident and couldn't. It was a small thing, and she couldn't remember it even happening. "So maybe I did. What's your point?"

"You smiled at Ralph. You helped him. You looked him in the eye. You treated him like a human being when almost no one else did. I knew who you were then. I knew you weren't just a pretty face, and I knew you were someone I wanted to know."

She was breathing heavily now, and her hands were shaking slightly. She twisted them together so Jeff wouldn't see. She wanted to believe him, but she wasn't sure she did. It sounded like a nice thing he was making up to make her feel better.

It did make her feel better.

"Why didn't you introduce yourself to me then, if you really wanted to get to know me?"

Jeff gave a wry chuckle. "Are you kidding me? You think I was the kind of guy who would just go up to a pretty girl and introduce myself? I was the kind of guy who got tongue-tied and ended up making a complete fool of himself."

She giggled. She couldn't help it. "You introduced yourself to me at the RUF meeting."

"Y-yeah. That's because you sat down right next to me. And it took all the courage I possessed, and I still think you thought I was pretty geeky."

She cleared her throat and tried to sober her expression.

"That's what I thought," he murmured. But his eyes were fond and amused, and he reached over and picked up one of her hands from her lap. "Vivian, nothing about my impression of you that very first day has been shown to be a lie. You're the warmest, most generous person I've ever met. You see people as humans, not as things to be used. You see into the heart of things. You see into the heart of me." His voice broke slightly, and he stopped talking.

She didn't want him to stop. She wanted to hear more. "I… It's nice of you to say that."

"I'm not being nice, Viv. I'm telling you the truth. The real you is the best, smartest, kindest, loveliest person I've ever met in my life. You don't have to pretend to be perfect and perfectly beautiful for people to love you. They're going to love you anyway."

She was trembling even more now, and she realized there were tears streaming out of her eyes. Since he was still holding one of her hands, she swiped them away quickly with the other.

There was no way Jeff hadn't seen the tears though.

"I'm not usually a crier," she said, giving him a wobbly smile.

"I know you're not." He was stroking her palm with his thumb, and the small touch sent shivers all the way through her.

"It must be lack of sleep," she added, telling herself to pull her hand away. He was making her feel things she shouldn't be feeling.

"I'm sure that's what it is," he said softly.

She liked the sound of his voice. And the way he seemed to really know her. And she really liked his touch.

She still hadn't pulled her hand away.

$\sim$

The rest of the day was a lot better. Jeff eventually left her room, and she was actually able to take a nap, so she was rested when she went to the pool later in the afternoon.

After dinner, they all went down to the beach and made a fire in one of the fire pits. They sat around it, drinking wine and roasting marshmallows and telling funny stories.

Vivian had a really good time. She didn't even miss her phone too much.

Jeff was sitting beside her, and they kept meeting each other's eyes, smiling or laughing. After about an hour, he'd slung an arm around her shoulders. It was just a companionable gesture. No one seemed to think a thing about it.

But it was starting to give Vivian wrong thoughts.

He looked cuter than ever in the moonlight and flickering firelight. Better than cute. Handsome. Masculine. Incredibly sexy.

She really shouldn't be thinking about him that way, but she couldn't help it. After a while, she started to get hit by increasing waves of attraction.

She wanted Jeff to tighten his grip on her.

She wanted him to start moving his hands.

She wanted him to touch her all over.

She wanted him to kiss her.

And all of it was totally wrong.

Eventually she was flushed and shaky and could no longer meet Jeff's eyes. Every time she looked at him, she would want him even more.

When his hand moved slightly, brushing her hair gently away from her neck, the jolt of pleasure and excitement that shot through her was too much for her to handle.

She cleared her throat and pulled away from him, telling the others that she was getting overly hot in the fire, so she was going to walk for a little while.

They all seemed to think her excuse was perfectly normal, so she was able to escape, breathing deeply in the sea breeze as she walked away.

Unfortunately, she heard footsteps right behind her.

She knew who it was, even before he fell in step with her.

She didn't look at him. Couldn't risk it.

"Viv," Jeff said, clearly trying to get her attention, get her to meet his eyes.

"What?" she said, staring out at the moonlight on the waves.

"Are you still mad at me?"

"Of course not."

"It feels like you're still mad at me, like you just remembered how I hurt you this morning."

"Well, I'm not," she said, wishing, willing, praying that he'd go away and leave her alone for a minute.

He reached out and put a hand on her upper arm, pulling her to a stop. "Viv, wait. I thought things were okay between us. I don't want you to be mad at me."

She let out a sigh that was almost a groan. "I said I wasn't mad."

"It feels like you are. Something's definitely wrong."

"Well, I'm not mad. You're reading this completely wrong. I'm not mad!" She looked up at him again and almost gulped at how handsome he looked in the soft light of the night, like some hero out of her fantasies.

Jeff wasn't supposed to be her hero.

He was the last man who could be her hero.

He reached up to brush her hair back from her face, searching her expression deeply. "You aren't?"

"No. I'm really not."

His expression changed, and she had no idea what he might have seen in her face. But he clearly didn't think she was angry anymore. His own features had softened, deepened, warmed.

He kept his hand on her face. "Good. I don't want you to be mad."

"I'm not," she murmured hoarsely.

He leaned in toward her, his eyes becoming hot all a sudden.

And she knew—she knew—he was going to kiss her, and it was the only thing she wanted in the world.

Then he suddenly jerked back and cleared his throat. "Good," he said, turning her around so they were walking back toward the fire. "If you're not mad, then come back and join the others."

She did what he said because it was safer that way, but she was brimming with emotion, with desire, and she was screaming inside at the loss of the kiss it had felt like she'd almost gotten.

It was better this way.

Clearly.

She couldn't go around and kiss Jeff.

But she really, really wanted to.

FOUR

Jeff had met his ex-wife, Kaylee, during his senior year in college. They'd been lab partners in biology, which he'd saved for his last year.

She'd been a sophomore, and she'd flirted with him all semester. He'd never taken it seriously, assuming she was using him to get a passing grade, as science was clearly not her subject. It wasn't his subject either, but he read well and memorized well and knew how to follow directions. He made As in everything in college, and biology was no exception. Kaylee had passed too because of his help.

He'd thought she was pretty but superficial, and he noticed she always shied away from Ralph in the dining hall. Maybe it wasn't fair to use this as a measuring stick for women, but he had ever since he'd first seen Vivian.

As he'd expected, as soon as the course was over, Kaylee had forgotten he'd existed. He might not socialize a lot, but he knew how to read people. He wasn't sad that a friendship or something more hadn't materialized.

He wanted a girl like Vivian, who was genuinely kind, who cared about other people and didn't just use them.

Vivian would obviously never look at him as a potential boyfriend, but he still wanted a girl like her.

He didn't think about Kaylee again. Not for four years.

The job he'd gotten after graduation was a remarkably good one, with a company he'd interned at for three summers in a row. The job paid well for someone his age, and he learned more than he could have imagined.

That year, he'd gotten a huge bonus because of the success of a project he'd worked on—and because the company had shown huge profits. He'd used that and some of his savings to buy a new car.

He'd bought a Mercedes in one of his few acts of indulgence. For the first time in his life, he could afford it, and the car would probably last him forever.

He'd just bought the car, when he'd decided to drive out to the homecoming football game at his old college. A lot of his old friends would be there. Vivian would be there—he knew because they'd connected on Facebook—and he wanted to talk to her about her blog, which now had a huge audience and potential for becoming a lot more.

He was getting out of his new car in one of his parking lots on campus when a female voice called out a greeting.

It was Kaylee, who'd graduated a couple of years back and was still working on campus in student services.

She was sweet and friendly and seemed genuinely glad to see him. She wanted to reconnect. She seemed to really listen when he talked, something she'd never done back in college, and she suggested they get together sometime for coffee.

She was interested in him. Really interested in him. She was pretty and outgoing and feminine, and she didn't appear nearly as superficial as she had been in college.

She'd grown up. She'd changed.

He'd really believed it was true.

Looking back, he knew what had happened. She'd seen his new car. That was what had prompted her interest. She'd believed he could afford to give her the lifestyle she wanted, and that had colored her impressions of him.

He hadn't known it back then though.

He'd been young and very stupid.

They'd dated for six months and were married in nine, and within the first year of marriage, Jeff was getting internal rumblings that everything wasn't right in their relationship.

Kaylee never seemed satisfied. She was always pushing him to spend more money, to change his wardrobe, to upgrade their apartment. Eventually they'd bought a huge house in one of the affluent Raleigh suburbs. It was a ridiculous house for a young couple with no kids, but Kaylee hadn't let up until he'd relented.

They had endless arguments about credit card bills and the ever-growing contents of Kaylee's walk-in closet.

He'd wanted to buy her a car shortly after they married (not a Mercedes—there was no way he could afford two), but none of the cars in their budget were acceptable to her, so she'd ended up leasing one instead.

She wanted an upgrade every year.

She wanted him to buy a new Mercedes, but his was only a few years old and he absolutely wasn't going to get a new one.

By then he'd partnered up with Vivian on Faith and Fabulousness, and for the first couple of years, there was no guarantee that the company would turn a profit. He literally could no longer afford to indulge Kaylee's spending habits. He'd had to put his foot down in a very unpleasant way.

That had been the end.

He wasn't what Kaylee had wanted after all.

One day, he came home to find that she'd packed up all her stuff—and a lot of stuff that had belonged to both of them—and had left him a note saying she wanted a divorce.

More than two years ago now.

He tried to reach out to her, see if there was any way to save their marriage. He obviously knew that marrying her had been a mistake, but he'd committed, and he didn't go back on his commitments. Not ever.

She wouldn't even talk to him. She certainly wouldn't agree to counseling or attempt a reconciliation. As soon as the divorce was finalized, she married a rich, much older man.

That was the life she wanted.

She'd never cheated on him. He was absolutely convinced that was true. She'd just never wanted *him*.

He wasn't going to make that mistake again even if it meant he remained unmarried for the rest of his life.

Some things were worse than occasionally being lonely. Some things were worse than not having sex.

Jeff was reminding himself of this truth—and his many mistakes in the past—the following morning over breakfast as he was watching Vivian laugh and tease Zeke.

She'd told him she was determined to get him to smile, and she was clearly making an effort.

Zeke remained unsmiling, although his blue eyes didn't look cold and hard. They looked like they were almost—almost—amused.

Vivian was beautiful this morning, as she always was, and she looked like she'd slept better last night. She'd been a little skittish with him this morning, and he wondered if it was because he'd almost kissed her last night.

That had been a mistake. He'd barely caught himself in time.

Then he'd spent half the night tossing and turning and thinking about Vivian. Half the time, he was trying futilely not to think about taking her to bed. The rest of the time was even worse—because it was his heart rather than his body doing the yearning. He was thinking about how vulnerable she'd been the day before when he'd come to her room to apologize. He wanted to hold her. He wanted to let her cry for real and know she was safe in his arms. He wanted to take care of her and show her how precious, how valuable she really was—for the rest of her life.

Very, very dangerous thoughts, and ones he hadn't even known he was foolish enough to feel.

He liked Vivian—better than anyone else in the world. He loved her even.

But he hadn't known he was in love with her. He hadn't thought he was that stupid.

He told himself he really wasn't. They were just passing feelings based on the intimacy he'd experienced with her yesterday.

Once this retreat was over, they'd get back to normal and he would no longer be tempted to do very foolish things.

He wasn't going to give his heart to another woman who would never really want it.

Vivian wasn't like Kaylee. He knew she wasn't. But she was beautiful and brilliant and successful and absolutely untouchable. She could have any man she wanted.

She wasn't going to want *him*.

~

They painted on canvases in the studio that morning, and then they went to the pool to play water polo.

Jeff enjoyed himself. He was absolutely terrible at painting, and Vivian made sure he knew it, but he was pretty good at polo, even in the water.

Vivian was a lot more confident today during the game, and so he didn't have to worry about her.

Except for watching her bounce around in her swimsuit with her wet, golden skin and her lush, curvy body.

He could have done without *that*.

They finished up a little before noon, and Vivian was still laughing as she climbed out of the pool.

As Jeff dried off, he tried to keep his eyes to himself, but they kept straying over to Vivian.

She was blotting her sopping wet hair, and water was streaming down her long, fit limbs. The wetness caused her red suit to cling to her body. She was in great shape, but she wasn't built like a model. She had rounded hips and full breasts and lean musculature in her arms and thighs. He could see the outline of her tight nipples through the wet fabric of the suit. Her breasts jiggled as she dried her hair.

He gulped as his whole body tightened with interest.

He could well imagine how her body would feel against his, how it would feel wrapped around him, how it would feel if he touched it, caressed her.

He wanted to so much that he was in danger of revealing his desire to other people, so he kept his towel positioned strategically.

She glanced over at him and saw him watching her, and she gave him a little smile.

She clearly had absolutely no idea what he was thinking.

She would probably be shocked and betrayed if she found out.

He tried to smile back but couldn't manage it since her expression made him visualize her smiling up at him in bed, all flushed and tousled and passionate.

He turned away from her quickly with a strangled sound.

Garrett came over and pounded him on the back. "Good game, man. It's not your fault that we were just the better team."

Jeff's team had lost.

Jeff tried to respond to the teasing but couldn't manage much. He was going to need to make an escape soon before someone started reading the signs.

So he announced they should all get showered and changed and reconvene for lunch in about a half hour.

Then he got upstairs before Vivian had finished toweling off.

~

He took a longer shower than normal, and he was just putting on his shoes when there was a knock on his door.

When he swung it open, he saw Vivian standing there, wearing a short knit dress that brought out the blue of her eyes and clung to her figure. She wasn't smiling and looked a little uncertain.

"Hey," he said. "I was just heading down." He finished with his shoes and glanced back over at her to see she was peering at him closely.

Shit. Surely she hadn't seen his physical response to her earlier.

He'd done everything in his power to hide it.

"What?" he said, a little more curtly than normal.

"Are you annoyed with me?"

He stared at her. "Of course not. Why would I be?"

"I don't know. You're just acting weird now, and you were acting kind of weird down by the pool."

She had noticed. She just hadn't known what was prompting it.

That was a grace in itself.

"No. Sorry, I was just distracted. Of course I'm not mad."

She stepped over closer to him, and her eyes were worried and soft on his face. "I really appreciate... yesterday. How you were with me. I hope you know that. How much I appreciate you. Because I do."

Shit, shit, shit—now his heart was responding as much as his body had earlier.

He just couldn't win.

He cleared his throat and looked down so she wouldn't see anything inappropriate in his eyes. "Thanks."

"Are you embarrassed?" Her voice was a little lighter now, more familiar.

That was as good an excuse as anything. "Uh, yeah."

She laughed. "You never could take a compliment." She reached out and wrapped her arms around him. "I adore you, Jeff. You know that, right?"

His heart shouldn't be soaring like this, thumping so fast it felt like it would literally leave the ground. He returned the hug, pulling her against him, and for a moment imagined he might have the right to hold her like this every day.

But her tone was almost teasing. She wasn't declaring her love for him.

She was being herself, being his friend, trying to make things comfortable between them again.

He managed to say, just a little hoarsely, "I'm kind of fond of you too."

She was smiling when he let her go, and he had to smile back.

She felt better, and he was sure pretty soon she would forget they'd even had this conversation.

He wouldn't forget though.

~

They were leaving after lunch when they ran into Cecily, who was showing a new couple around the center.

She smiled at them and said, "Hello, Vivian, Jeff. Let me introduce you. The Duncans have just arrived to stay for a few days. This is Daniel and Jessica."

The Duncans looked to be in their thirties. Jessica was tall, slim, and attractive in an understated way—not bright and stylish like Vivian. And Daniel had dark hair, a friendly smile, and an intelligent look about him.

They introduced themselves, saying they were from the mountains in the western part of the state. Daniel was a pastor, and they were the parents of a toddler, who was staying with his aunt and uncle while his parents had a little break.

Vivian was her normal outgoing self, asking a lot of questions and clearly making the couple like her and want to get to know her better. She did it without even trying to. It was just one of her gifts.

Jeff wasn't like that, so he appreciated it in others.

After they'd talked for about ten minutes, they said their goodbyes, and Vivian and Jeff started back upstairs.

"They seem nice," Vivian said, leaning back against the rail in the elevator.

"Yeah."

They were silent for a minute as the elevator ascended. When the doors slid open, Vivian asked, "What are you going to do this afternoon?"

"I don't know. I hadn't thought about it. What about you?"

"I don't know." Vivian was standing in the hallway in front of her room, and she shifted from leg to leg.

"You can go lie by the pool. Or out on the beach?"

"I've done that for the past two days."

"A lot of people like to do it every day."

She gave a little shrug.

"What's the matter?" he asked.

"I don't know. I just feel kind of... restless, you know. I want to do something."

"You're here to relax."

"I know, but it's boring to relax for too long. I don't feel like reading or napping. I want to *do* something."

Jeff wanted to do something too, but he was pretty sure that wasn't what Vivian meant.

"Well, get some exercise or something. If you're tired enough, you won't be restless."

"Yeah."

"Why don't you take a run? It's not too hot today, and you could run on the beach."

"Yeah. I guess."

"Why do you guess? Isn't running your thing?"

"It is. I usually like it."

"So what's the problem?"

"I wanted to do something with someone else," she said, looking unusually shy.

His heart did the silliest little flip-flop as he wondered if she was hinting at him to join her.

Maybe that was why she seemed so strangely undecided.

"I can come with you if you want," he offered, trying to sound casual.

Her eyes shot up to his face, and she broke out in a smile.

That was what she'd wanted.

She'd wanted to do something with *him*.

"But you're not a runner," she said.

He gave a half shrug. "I can run. I'm in decent shape, you know."

"I know you are. I just meant, you don't like to run."

"How do you know?"

"I've never known you to run before."

"Well, I am now. So go change clothes and meet back here in five minutes." He spoke brusquely because he was trying to hide how excited he was about her desire to hang out with him.

"Five minutes! How am I supposed to change clothes that quickly?"

"How long does it take? No primping. Five minutes."

She grumbled under her breath as she opened her door, but he suspected she was smiling.

So was he.

~

Jeff worked out semiregularly, but he wasn't any sort of athlete and he never did much running.

He should have thought of this before he'd suggested running with Vivian.

She ran several times a week. She was just better at it than him. He did fine to begin with, but soon he was out of breath, and the sun was beating down on him with oppressive heat. And then his body started to hurt—mostly his knees and calves. And eventually it felt like his blood was throbbing so painfully it was going to burst out of his body.

Vivian, naturally, looked perfectly fine—flushed and with a sheen of perspiration on her skin but breathing evenly and still running at a steady pace.

Jeff could barely see through the sweat pouring into his eyes, and he was afraid any minute he would just collapse onto the hot sand.

And Vivian would know how unimpressive he really was.

"You want to take a break?" she asked, her voice slightly breathless but otherwise normal.

He looked over at her, and she nodded toward a bench in front of them.

He would have liked to say he didn't need one but better to rest now than to completely humiliate himself. "Sure," he said, attempting casual.

They slowed to a walk as they headed to the bench, and Jeff's legs were so shaky that his knees almost buckled as he sat down.

It should have been better now that he was sitting, but heat seemed to rise like a wave inside him, from his belly to his chest to his head. He could hardly breathe around the heat.

He had to lean over and gasp loudly until he was able to take in air normally again.

When he straightened up and wiped away the sweat, he saw that Vivian was watching him. Her lips were trembling, and her eyes were dancing.

He groaned. "Don't say it."

She laughed out loud. "I thought you said you could run."

"I can run. I ran all this way, didn't I?"

"And you look like you're about to pass out."

He groaned again, but the breath caught in his throat, so he had to lean forward and breathe deeply again.

Vivian was still laughing as she got up and walked over to a food stand and then returned with a bottle of water. She took a sip and then handed it to him.

He started with small sips until the heat in his body started to subside. Then he took a few larger gulps.

He was feeling better when Vivian reached for the bottle and finished it off.

Jeff dropped his head in his hands. "Well, that was embarrassing."

Vivian laughed again and reached out to rub his back. His shirt was almost soaked with sweat, but it didn't stop her from touching him. "We could have done something other than run," she said. "I'm sorry I made you."

"Don't be sorry. I thought it would be easier than this."

"Running on the sand isn't easy."

"You didn't seem to have much trouble with it."

"I run all the time."

"I *hate* running," he grumbled. "The entire purpose of existence for the torturous activity seems to be humiliating me and making me suffer."

She laughed again and scooted closer, leaning her face against his shoulder. "I don't think running has a personal grudge against you."

"Yes, it does. For Pete's sake."

He heard the last words as they came out of his lips, and he shot his eyes over to Vivian's face. He saw her lips wobble in suppressed amusement.

She obviously saw that he saw, so she laughed out loud. "I haven't heard you say that in a while."

He hadn't used the expression since she'd mentioned it. He didn't even know why—just that he didn't want to be a source of amusement for her.

He wanted her to... admire him, respect him.

Want him.

Her laughter faded as she watched his face. "You haven't been stopping yourself from saying it because of me, have you?"

He just rolled his eyes at her, partly because he still hadn't caught his breath and partly because he didn't know what to say.

She'd straightened up as they talked, but now she leaned against him again. "I didn't want you to stop saying it. I like that you say it. It feels like... you. And I like it."

"You like that I sound like I should be a neighbor of Beaver Cleaver?" he asked dryly.

"Yes. I like it. It's… you."

Despite his complaints, his rueful embarrassment was quickly transforming to very different feelings. She felt so sweet and fond, leaning against him that way. She didn't seem to care that he was red and sweaty and still out of breath. And she appeared to mean what she said about liking even the parts of him that were kind of dorky.

She seemed to want to be close to him.

He couldn't help but raise his hand and brush back the loose hairs that had escaped her ponytail.

She looked up at him at his touch. Either she saw something in his eyes or a new thought had flickered through her head, because her smile faded to something deep, serious, hotter than warm.

She was flushed and sweating and strong and feminine and vibrant and everything he wanted.

And he was too tired to hold himself back. He raised a hand to her face, cupping it gently.

She sucked in a breath, and her lips parted slightly. Her tongue darted out to moisten her lips.

His whole body throbbed with one simple truth. This woman was for him.

He leaned toward her, and she wasn't pulling away. She was going to let him kiss her. His eyes blurred over with the realization.

At the very last minute, he remembered that she was Vivian Harper, and she was never going to want more than a kiss from him.

He pulled back rather awkwardly.

Vivian's brows lowered, and she took a ragged breath.

Jeff felt like a fool, and he hated himself for not taking what his body and heart were both crying out for.

He thought Vivian would stand up, regain her usual self, suggest they return to Balm in Gilead.

Instead, she said softly, "That's the second time you almost kissed me."

She'd always been direct. One of the many things he loved about her.

He had no idea what to say, so he didn't say anything.

"Are you ever going to do it for real?" she added.

His eyes shot back to her face. She was looking at him expectantly. She smelled like salt and sunshine and effort and sunscreen and the melon-scented lotion she used.

He let out a soft groan and took her face in his hand again, leaning forward to claim her lips with his.

His body pulsed with pleasure as he tasted her at last, as her whole body softened into the kiss. Her hand came up to tangle in his hair, and her lips moved eagerly against his, like he was a dessert she couldn't wait to finish.

His body started to respond to the roar in his head, in his heart. He felt himself starting to harden, and the knowledge forced him to pull away.

She didn't want to stop kissing him. She let out a little whimper and followed his retreat, holding on to his neck with both hands, her mouth clinging deliciously to his.

"Vivian," he murmured, his voice ridiculously thick. He slid one of his hands down her back, feeling the smooth curve of her spine, the irresistible softness of her bottom.

She let out a long breath as she finally pulled her lips away from his. He rested his forehead against hers.

"That was... that was..." She was more breathless now than she'd been after the run.

He was afraid she was going to say it had been a huge mistake. And he would be crushed because kissing her felt like the best thing he'd ever done in his life.

Like one of the things he'd been created to do.

"That was really good," she concluded at last.

"It was better than good."

Her eyes darted up to his, and then she dropped her gaze again, looking soft and pretty and slightly shy and more irresistible than ever.

"Then maybe we'll have to do it again," she replied.

That was exactly what Jeff wanted to hear.

FIVE

The first boy Vivian kissed was her high school boyfriend. She'd just turned sixteen, and he'd taken her out for pizza and a movie. They'd stood on her front porch afterward, and he'd leaned forward a little awkwardly, bumping her with his nose.

He'd kissed her for exactly three seconds.

She knew because she'd counted.

She'd dated him all through high school, and she'd assumed she'd marry him and they'd keep living in the small North Carolina town where they'd both grown up. But he'd broken up with her right after graduation, explaining as nicely as he could that he'd always felt like they were just a high school thing and she didn't really want him for the long haul.

She'd cried for two days, but then she'd shrugged it off and started to focus on heading in the fall to the Christian college she'd always wanted to attend. And underneath the hurt, a small part of her was relieved.

She liked her hometown, and she'd thought she'd loved that boy.

But now she was free. Nothing would be holding her in this one small world.

She'd dated three different guys in college, each relationship lasting at least six months. With each one, she'd assumed there might be a future, but the guys had each ended up dumping her with various explanations that they just weren't right for each other.

Every time, she'd cried. And every time, she'd had that little flicker of relief.

Since she'd gotten out of college, she'd dated semiregularly. Most of the time, the relationships were just casual—just someone to go out with, go to social events with. A few men she'd thought had real potential.

The last man she'd kissed was sixteen months ago. He'd been a hotshot defense attorney in Raleigh—smart, handsome, and ambitious. They'd dated for about four months when he just stopped calling her.

After a week, she'd called him to check in, and he'd explained it wasn't going to work out. He didn't feel like she really needed him, and he wanted a woman who did.

His words were so close to the words of her first boyfriend that they'd hit her hard.

She liked men. She genuinely wanted to get married. She wasn't unhappy as she was—at all—but marriage was something she still dreamed on. Maybe children. She wasn't sure about that. But definitely marriage.

Somehow though, she was giving off vibes that told men she wasn't interested.

And she didn't know why, and she didn't know how to fix it.

She hadn't dated much since. It felt like a futile exercise if she was somehow sabotaging herself. Her friends told her she was just too confident and successful—and that was intimidating to most men—but she saw other successful women find men who wanted to marry them.

She was somehow turning men away, and she couldn't help but wonder if it had something to do with that tiny flicker of relief she felt every time they broke up with her.

Now there was Jeff.

She had no idea what was happening there, but she'd been reliving that kiss over and over again throughout the night, and she was still thinking about it as she showered and dressed the next morning with a giddiness she hadn't felt in a really long time.

She was so wired that she finished dressing early and went down to the pool deck to get some fresh air and listen to the ocean.

She wondered what Jeff would say when he saw her today.

She wondered what he would look like.

She wondered if he would kiss her again.

She was walking back inside when an arm reached out from around the corner of the hallway and pulled her out of the lobby and back against a wall.

She huffed in surprise but couldn't hold back a flash of excitement when she realized it was Jeff. He was leaning her against the wall, a little smile on his face.

"What was that for?" she asked breathlessly. Her hands had gone up of their own accord to fist in his red golf shirt. "You startled me."

"I knocked on your door to walk down with you to breakfast, and you weren't there. Are you trying to hide from me?" he asked, his brown eyes soft and hot and fond.

"No. Of course not. I was just getting some air. I was ready early and felt... restless."

"Did you?" He leaned closer to her, his body warmth causing her to flush. "Are you sure you're not trying to avoid me?"

She lowered her eyes, feeling ridiculously shy. She had no idea why. This was Jeff—her partner for a long time—but she'd never seen him like this before.

She liked it. A lot.

"I'm not trying to avoid you," she said, raising her eyes and getting another thrill from his expression. "I promise."

"Good," he murmured. He cupped her face with one hand the way he had yesterday and brushed her lips with his. Just the slightest touch. So delicious. "I was afraid you might have decided this was a mistake."

"No. I don't think so. Or I guess I don't really know. Maybe it is, but it doesn't feel like it. It... I don't even know." She was never so inarticulate. She couldn't even get a full sentence out.

"We don't have to know everything right now," he said, his expression changing to the slightly earnest seriousness that was so much a part of him. "As long as you're okay with me kissing you occasionally."

Her mouth twitched up in a little smile. "I think I could live with that."

"Good." He kissed her again, just a little more than the first brush of his lips but nothing hot and heavy. "Then I will. Keep kissing you, I mean."

She experienced a sudden jolt of fear, of self-consciousness, as she imagined what everyone else would think if they saw Jeff kissing her.

They'd assume it was serious.

They'd assume they would be getting married very soon.

And there was no reason to assume that would ever happen between her and Jeff. After all, her luck with men was inevitably bad.

She could suddenly picture herself walking into the office and having to tell the rest of the staff that Jeff had broken up with her, that he hadn't really wanted her after all.

The visual was so nauseating that her breath caught in her throat.

"What's the matter?" he asked, studying her expression.

"Nothing. Not really. I'm just wondering... Maybe we should keep this... keep it private. Not go public with the kissing thing. Yet."

It would be so much safer that way. If Jeff decided he didn't want this, then she'd be the only person to know.

His forehead wrinkled slightly, and she could see him thinking through the words, processing what they meant, working through all the implications. "That would be fine," he said slowly, after several seconds.

"I'm just worried—about it interfering with work."

"How would it interfere with work?" He didn't sound annoyed or resistant. Just like he was still figuring it out.

"It would feel strange and awkward. Everyone would be talking about us and watching us and teasing us. It would get in the way. Please?"

Jeff nodded. "Of course. Of course we can keep it private for now."

She exhaled in a gust of relief and slipped her hands up to the back of his head, tugging on his thick hair just a little. He responded by kissing her again, teasing her bottom lip very gently with his tongue for a few seconds before pulling away.

They smiled at each other like naughty children with a fun, sneaky plan, and then he put a hand on the small of her back as they started in toward breakfast. He kept his hand on her back until they'd cleared the hallway, and then he let his hand drop.

They walked into the dining room side by side but not touching at all.

~

The morning passed as the three previous mornings had—with physical and creative activities as a group. But throughout the hours, Vivian kept letting her eyes slip over to Jeff, and they'd share secret looks that made her want to hug herself.

What the hell was happening here?

This was Jeff. And she'd never imagined feeling things like this for him before.

But she was. She definitely was.

And she didn't even want them to go away.

If they could be careful about it, then maybe they could work things out in a way that wouldn't distract either of them or the rest of the team from the work they needed to do.

If they were careful, maybe this could continue—even after this week was over.

After lunch, she went down to lie by the pool with a book. She assumed Jeff would come to join her since she'd told him that was where she would be, but she'd been down for ten minutes and still hadn't seen a glimpse of him.

What was he doing?

Why wasn't he coming to join her?

Had he already decided doing something else was better than being with her?

She pushed the thoughts aside since they were silly and irrational and wondered if she should go look for him. She was still internally debating when a woman came over to sit in the chaise beside her.

It was Jessica Duncan, the woman she'd met yesterday.

Vivian smiled at her with genuine friendliness, although her mind was still distracted with Jeff's location.

Jessica was wearing a cute blue tankini with a little skirt around the bottom—like the ones they sold in popular mail-order catalogs that were supposed to hide figure flaws. Vivian didn't think Jessica needed it. She looked intelligent and quiet and attractive. Vivian had liked her right away.

"Okay," Jessica said, taking off her sunglasses as she looked over at Vivian. "I have to ask."

Vivian blinked. "Ask what?"

"Are you Vivian Harper from Faith and Fabulousness?"

Despite the fact that her company was quite successful, Vivian wasn't anything like a celebrity. Only in Christian circles was she occasionally recognized and usually just then because they'd heard the name and didn't immediately identify her face.

She hadn't told Jessica her last name yesterday, so the other woman had clearly recognized her by appearance.

"Yes," she said with a surprised smile. "I am. You know it?"

"Of course I know it! I've been following you since you were just doing the blog. I'm so excited to get to meet you!" Jessica's eyes were utterly genuine. She didn't have any sort of agenda. She meant what she was saying.

"Okay—that makes me feel really great," Vivian admitted with a smile.

"It must happen all the time to you. I mean, I see Faith and Fabulousness everywhere."

"It really doesn't happen all the time. We've been doing very well, but people mostly just know the name itself and don't know me by sight. And—I don't mean to sound cynical or anything—but a lot of people who reach out to me seem to have some sort of agenda, like they're looking for something from me."

"I can believe it. I guess it goes with success. But I've seriously been following you from the beginning. The first post I read from you was about your trip to Quebec, back when you were in college. You had all those amazing photos you'd taken, and you were reflecting about travel and history and tradition and faith and the Bible, and I literally cried over it." Jessica looked almost rueful. "I really did."

Maybe because she'd been feeling a little insecure lately, but the other woman's words struck a powerful note in her heart. She felt her own eyes swelling slightly, blurring her vision. "Wow. Thanks. Thanks for telling me. I'm so glad."

"My husband bought me the book on shoes for my birthday. I'm not a shoe person or a clothes person or anything. I'm as low maintenance as you can get. But I loved that book so much. The photography was stunning, of course, but it was some of those little written reflections that got me. You must have written some of them. I know your name wasn't on the book, but I'm sure I recognized your voice on some of them." She paused for a moment. "The best ones."

Vivian swallowed hard. She had no idea what was wrong with her, but it felt like she was about to cry. "I... I added a little," she admitted. "I'm so glad you loved the book."

"You have no idea how much Daniel teased me about my spending all that time reading about shoes, after I've spent years telling him I don't care about fashion at all." Jessica laughed. "I thought I'd never hear the end of it. And there's no way I'll ever admit to him that I really wanted to buy a pair of great shoes after I'd finished the book."

Vivian laughed too, managing to pull herself together. "Did you buy some?"

"No. But maybe I should have."

"You definitely should have." Vivian was about to say something else when she was aware of a presence standing beside her.

She shaded her eyes against the sun and looked up to discover Jeff. He was taking off his shirt, and she was momentarily distracted by the sight of his bare chest.

He wasn't built big or bulky, but he was in good shape overall. And his chest was very nice, very masculine. She really liked the look of it.

"I was wondering where you were."

"I had a phone call," he explained with an intimate little twitch of his lips.

"With what phone?" She was momentarily outraged by the idea of his having a phone when he'd taken hers away.

"The landline here. I didn't sneak in a phone like some people I can mention." He was teasing her. It was clear from his voice.

She really liked the sound of it.

Remembering where she was, she turned back to Jessica, who was also smiling. "I remember Jeff from yesterday," she said, giving him a little wave as he stretched out in the chaise next to Vivian's. "Are you two... together, as well as business partners?"

The question was blunt but not rude. Jessica was genuinely interested, and there was a kindness underlying the smile.

But the question took Vivian aback, and she had no idea how to answer it.

They were kind of together right now. At least, they were kissing.

But they also weren't announcing it to the world.

Vivian cleared her throat. "We've... we've always been friends. We went to college together."

That was true, and it could act as an answer without revealing too much. It was the best she could do.

She glanced over at Jeff, and she saw his eyes were on her face. His expression had changed—it wasn't quite as teasing and fond—but she wasn't sure how to read it.

Surely he didn't expect her to announce to a stranger that they'd started kissing yesterday.

Talk about inappropriate.

Maybe he felt a little uncomfortable with the situation too—just like she did. That might explain his altered expression.

~

That evening, they all went down to the beach again. Garrett brought his guitar with him, and they sat around the fire pit, chatted, and sang old hymns and favorite praise songs.

Vivian had a really good time. She loved these people, and she loved the little looks she occasionally shared with Jeff.

It made her feel special in a way she didn't always feel.

She tried not to look at him too much, afraid to give something away to the others. But every time her eyes slipped over to him, his eyes were resting on her face.

His finely chiseled features looked starkly handsome in the firelight, and his hair blazed with gold. He was like some kind of Greek god, come down to earth just for her.

It was a ridiculous thought. He was still Jeff. The same old Jeff she'd always liked so much but who had never taken her breath away.

She didn't know why he was taking her breath away now.

After about an hour, she was starting to feel too hot in front of the fire and too jittery with the way Jeff kept looking at her.

There was a strange kind of pressure behind his regard—as if he believed she was better than she really was—and it made her nervous, jittery.

Guys admired her often enough. They told her they thought she was pretty.

But as soon as she started getting close to them, they would inevitably break up with her.

She wondered when it would happen with Jeff.

She told the others she needed to stretch her legs and went to take a walk on the beach by herself.

She couldn't help but wonder if Jeff would join her. She wanted him to and was afraid he would at the same time.

She'd been walking about five minutes when he caught up with her.

He reached to take her hand. "Are you trying to get away from me?" he asked, falling in step with her.

"No! Of course not."

He watched her closely in the moonlight and starlight. "Then you were hoping to sneak away with me for a few minutes?"

She chuckled, squeezing his hand. "Not exactly. I'm not complaining at all, but I really just wanted to stretch my legs."

She expected him to let her hand slip out of his now that they were walking together, but he didn't. He held it in a close but not hard grip.

She loved how it felt. Possessive. Intimate. Like the clasp of his hand was claiming her as his and him as hers.

But it also made her feel weird and jumpy.

This wasn't something she normally did—walking on the beach, holding hands with a man.

"Who was your call from this afternoon?" she asked after a few minutes of silence. She'd almost forgotten about that detail in the hours since he'd mentioned it. She wasn't sure why it occurred to her now.

"Hannah."

She straightened up. Hannah was one of their interns manning the office this week. "Is something wrong?"

"No. I'd called this morning to check and make sure they didn't have any questions, and she was just calling back. Nothing is going on. They have it all under control."

"I thought we weren't supposed to be thinking about work this week," she said, narrowing her eyes at him. "Have you been sneaking in some work behind my back?"

He laughed. "No. I just thought it was safer to check in. They're good, but they're still in college. Even if they're just covering the phones, email, and social media, who knows what might happen in a week. And I didn't want you to be worrying about it."

She felt almost ashamed that she hadn't even thought about work at all today. Her mind had been filled with other things. "Oh. Okay."

"What's the matter?" he asked softly, evidently seeing something in her face.

"Nothing." She smiled up at him. "Really nothing. I was just... You don't have to worry about me."

He stopped walking and turned her to face him. "Well, I do worry about you. I like to take care of you. It feels like my special privilege."

He was so sweet and earnest and genuine. He'd always been all those things, but it felt different now that he was directing it toward her personally.

She loved it. So much. And it still terrified her.

She was filled with flutters as she smiled up at him. "I don't need taking care of."

"Everyone needs taking care of."

"What about you?"

He gently pushed her hair back from her face, where the wind had blown it. "I wouldn't complain if you decided you wanted to take care of me."

"Oh really?"

"Yes, really." He leaned down to kiss her, still holding her hand. It felt so good she pressed herself against the lean, hard line of his body. When he pulled his lips away, his face still a breath away from hers, he murmured, "But I'll want to take care of you even if you never want to take care of me."

Her heart felt like it might explode from the flood of feeling rushing through it. She had no idea what to say to that, what to do. She rested her cheek on his shoulder for a minute, one of his arms around her waist and their hands still clasped together.

Finally she said softly, "I... I never knew you felt this way."

"Neither did I," he admitted. "Oh, I guess I've had inklings of all this for the past year or so, but I was trying to ignore it. But some things just can't be ignored forever."

That was true.

She knew it herself.

She'd never known or admitted that she wanted to walk along the beach, holding Jeff's hand.

But evidently she had.

SIX

Jeff woke up hard.

He'd actually slept pretty well for the most part, only waking up a couple of times to chaotic, excited thoughts about Vivian. But at six thirty the following morning, he opened his eyes to the knowledge that his body was throbbing with unsatisfied physical desire.

He was hot, sweating, flushed, uncomfortable—and very, very hard.

He rolled out of bed with a groan and limped to the shower. After turning it on much cooler than was comfortable, he stepped in and dealt with the painful shock of the cold spray hitting his hot skin.

He hadn't had sex since Kaylee had left. Dealing with physical frustration was commonplace for him. But it wasn't usually this intense.

He'd always been attracted to Vivian, but in the past four days, something had changed. All his yearning, all his passion, all his primitive biological urges had coalesced into one unstoppable force, focused only on her.

It wasn't good.

It wasn't good at all.

Kissing her was good—better than anything. And the fact that she wanted to kiss him back was like a miracle.

But she hadn't suddenly discovered he was the love of her life. He was absolutely convinced she was just trying something out, indulging this sudden new whimsy. She didn't want anyone else to know about it, and that was because she wasn't sure this would last. There was no reason to assume or expect this would continue for longer than the week. He'd be an utter fool to let himself believe she was already serious about it.

And if he couldn't get his head and heart and body reined in where she was concerned, he would be utterly devastated when she returned to the office and remembered who she was and what was most important to her.

She'd insisted on keeping the change in relationship secret from the staff. She'd told Jessica Duncan yesterday that she and Jeff were just friends.

She was definitely playing it safe here, and Jeff needed to do the same.

But even with this piece of wisdom and the cold shower, it was several minutes before he had himself under control enough to pray.

For years now Jeff had made a point of praying in the shower and on his daily commutes in the car. They were built-in times every day when he was required to perform fairly mindless activities and couldn't do anything else. As he scrubbed his body and washed his hair and waited at traffic lights, he would talk to God and try to listen.

But this morning it was several minutes before he was able to concentrate on praying.

~

The morning passed as the other mornings had—in generally enjoyable team activities. He didn't even mind that in the midst of their tennis game they ended up brainstorming about a web series devoted to gardens. And he tried not to obsess over every time Vivian wouldn't meet his eyes.

This was new for her—just like him. And she was used to being completely confident in who she was and how she interacted with her staff. Of course, she was a little insecure about how she would behave with him right now in front of the others.

Yes, she was a little skittish, but that didn't mean she was second-guessing things between them.

It didn't mean she wanted to stop kissing him.

It didn't mean there was nothing else between them *but* kissing.

He caught her in the lobby after lunch and pulled her into a quiet hallway.

She was breathing quickly as she stared up at him, and her eyes were very wide.

She was nervous. He could see it. It did something strange to his heart.

"What is it?" she asked, when he didn't say anything.

"Did you want to do something this afternoon?"

She gave him a little smile. "I assumed I'd do something."

"I meant with me."

"I knew what you meant."

"Maybe we can go out somewhere so we're not at risk of being seen."

She nodded, and he could feel her relax, as if she liked the safety his suggestion offered. "I wouldn't mind going shopping."

"Why did I know you were going to say that?"

"Don't be snide." She started to touch his chest in an affectionate gesture but dropped her hand. "We can do something else if you'd rather."

"Shopping is fine. Do you think there's anything here but those tacky beach shops?"

"We can drive through several towns and check them out," Vivian said. Her whole demeanor had brightened, and he'd always loved when that happened—like joy was bursting out of her so intensely that it spilled out of all her pores. "I'm kind of hot and sweaty, so I might take a shower and change first though."

"That's fine. I'll wait for you down here."

She touched his arm gently before she turned around and returned to the lobby.

Jeff again reminded himself not to get too excited about this.

They'd always gotten along.

They'd always cared for each other.

It was new and promising that she'd now discovered that she could view him as a man, but that didn't mean she'd made any sort of commitment or decision.

He'd been down the road of pouring himself into a relationship with a woman who didn't want him.

He knew better than to do that again.

He just had to keep reminding himself.

Seeking a distraction, he wandered outside onto the pool deck and went to stand by the railings, looking at the waves come in and out. It wasn't as sunny today as it had been earlier that week, and the clouds made the water look sober, serious, reflective—with only the occasional sparkle flashing out.

"They say it's not going to rain," a voice came from behind him. "But it sure looks like it will."

Jeff turned around and saw Daniel Duncan, whom he'd met two days ago. Jessica's husband. A preacher. That was all Jeff knew about the other man. He smiled since Daniel had sounded friendly. "Hopefully the clouds will blow out of here soon." He glanced around but saw no sign of Daniel's wife. "You're on your own?"

"Jessica's upstairs changing. I'm just waiting."

"So am I," Jeff admitted. "I guess guys do a lot of that."

Daniel chuckled and came forward to stand next to Jeff at the railing. "Jessica is actually really fast at changing clothes and getting ready, but my first wife used to take longer. Oh the hours I spent waiting."

Daniel's tone was fond, so it was clear he didn't hold any resentment against his first wife's slow beauty routine, but Jeff's eyebrows lifted at this piece of information. He never would have guessed that Daniel had been divorced. He came across as the kind of man who would marry young and stay married his entire life.

Of course, Jeff had always assumed he was one of those men too.

Life didn't always happen the way you expected.

"So you're divorced too?" Jeff asked because he was genuinely curious and Daniel seemed fairly open and forthcoming.

Daniel's face sobered slightly. "No. My first wife died."

Jeff felt a jolt of surprise—and then guilt. Here he was, thinking about himself and how he was glad he wasn't the only one whose wife walked out on him, when Daniel had had to deal with the death of a spouse. "Oh. I'm sorry to hear that."

Daniel gave a half shrug. "Thanks. It was a really good marriage—just a short one. It's been several years. I have Jessica now—and a son. God is good." He paused for a few seconds. "When did you get divorced?"

"Officially, it's been a little over a year, but she left me more than two years ago." Jeff wasn't usually the kind of person who spilled a lot of personal information to strangers, but it felt easy to talk to Daniel, and for some reason he wanted to.

"That had to be hard. I would imagine, even if you can see things working out in good ways afterward, going through it had to be really painful."

"Yeah. I tried. I really did. But there are some things that just can't be fixed. I guess."

Daniel nodded. "Yes. But *we* can be fixed. I find that a very encouraging thought."

The words struck Jeff unexpectedly, and he was silent as he thought them through.

His marriage hadn't been fixable—at least not on his own. It had left him broken in a lot of ways he was still trying to work through.

But he was fixable. God could fix him.

Here was Daniel, obviously in love with his wife and his family and the life he was living—even though his first wife had been taken in a way that must have felt very cruel.

Maybe there was hope for Jeff too.

Maybe there could be a future with Vivian beyond kissing in hidden corners.

It wasn't a sure thing, but it was a possibility.

Maybe Jeff should treat it as a possibility.

His heart was beating quickly when Vivian came out of the building and out onto the pool deck.

She smiled when she met his eyes and waved. "There you are! I was looking for you."

Jeff felt his mouth, his face, his whole being smiling in response.

He'd been looking for her too.

~

They drove south toward Ocracoke and stopped in each little town they came to. Despite its growing popularity, the Outer Banks weren't very commercialized yet, so the shopping options were mostly beach shops and little grocery stores. But they found a couple of cute markets and had fun browsing local food items and crafts.

Most of the stores were what Vivian called "primitive shops" and what Jeff called "junk stores." Vivian obviously loved this kind of shopping as much as she did shopping for designer clothes, and Jeff just loved watching her enjoy it.

After about an hour, Vivian suggested they stop somewhere for a drink, so they went to sit on the outdoor patio of a local coffee shop. Vivian got an herbal tea and a sugar cookie. Jeff got a beer.

As they sat, twice he saw Vivian reach for her purse and then stop abruptly. He knew what she was doing.

Looking for her phone.

He found himself doing the same thing more often than he'd expected. It was habit—second nature—to check in, to look for messages, to find out what was happening in the world.

The second time she reached for her phone, Vivian caught him looking at her and gave him a wry smile. "Sometimes I try to remember what it was like as a kid, when

I didn't always have a phone, and I really can't even remember."

"I can't either," he admitted. "It really is a kind of miracle—carrying a computer around in our pockets the way we do now. Kaylee used to..." He trailed off as he realized what he was saying.

She cocked her head slightly and said after a brief pause, "Kaylee used to what?"

He gave a little shrug. "Nothing."

"You don't talk about her much."

"I know."

"You can, you know. I wouldn't mind." She sipped her tea and added with downcast eyes, "I'd like for you to be able to talk about her to me."

It meant something—that she said that, that she clearly meant it. Jeff cleared his throat. "I... Thanks. It's just that I don't want to be one of those guys who are always whining and complaining about his ex-wife."

She lifted her eyes to meet his. "You can talk to me about her without whining and complaining."

"Maybe. But honestly I wouldn't always have nice things to say about her. I guess we had our moments—a few of them—but it wasn't a good marriage."

"I know." Her voice was soft as if she were afraid of startling or unnerving him.

He glanced away, feeling embarrassed for no good reason. "It happens. Everyone makes mistakes. But sometimes you make a mistake that you have to pay for—for years."

"But it's over now, isn't it? You're not still paying for it, are you?"

"Not really. I never see or talk to her anymore, and since we didn't have any kids, there was nothing tying us together. The only thing that's left is…" He trailed off again, this time not because he didn't want to speak ill of Kaylee but rather because he didn't want Vivian to think he was foolish.

"Is what?" she prompted, her eyes very soft on his face. "All the emotional stuff?"

He nodded. "I'm over the worst of it. I really am. But it's surprising sometimes how much lingers—well past the time when it should."

She nodded, clearly thinking through what he'd said. "I guess maybe it's hard for you to trust women now."

"Not as a whole, but…" He cleared his throat again, wishing he could be more in control and articulate. He couldn't though. This went too deep—and his feelings for Vivian did too. "It's just that I… I gave Kaylee my heart, and she just didn't want it. It's hard not to assume it's going to happen again."

"I can understand that. That's got to be normal, after what you went through." She was silent for a minute before she asked in a different voice, "You trust me, don't you?"

His eyes shot over to her face, and he saw that the idea that he might not really bothered her. He reached over to take her hand, holding it on the table. "Of course I trust you, Viv."

"I hope you do. You're so incredibly special to me, Jeff."

His throat ached with feeling as he squeezed her hand. "I do trust you. We've known each other so long. We've had so many years together. I do trust you. It's not the same as it was with Kaylee."

He knew this was true, and somehow saying it out loud made it feel more true.

He'd been wrong about Kaylee, but he wasn't wrong about Vivian.

He'd known her for thirteen years, and his first impression of her—in that orientation event—had been proven right over and over again.

She gave him a little smile. "I trust you too."

~

They kept moving through a few little towns after their break, and they visited four other stores. When he needed to make a quick bathroom break, he came out to see Vivian standing over a little wooden table in the corner of the seventh cluttered shop of the afternoon.

Even on first glance, Jeff knew that something had changed in her mood. She'd been bright and laughing all day—except for their conversation at the coffee shop—but she wasn't smiling now. She was staring down at the vintage table with a strangely deep, quiet look on her face.

He walked over and put a hand on her back.

She glanced up with a little smile but then turned back to the table. It looked about fifty years old and was obviously made as a side table for a chair. It had a small flat surface, one shelf underneath, and four thin, delicate legs. It had obviously been painted more than once in its history, and the brown, green, and white paints were visible in different areas, giving a kind of shabby chic look to the thing.

"You okay?" he asked, rubbing her back gently and amazed that he was able to do so, that she was letting him do so.

"Yeah," she said. There was a break in her voice though. "Isn't it beautiful?"

He turned back to the table. Surely she wasn't getting all emotional over this old thing? It was cute enough, but pieces like this were a dime a dozen in these kinds of junk stores. "It's okay, I guess. It needs to be sanded and re-stained though."

"No!" She stroked the rough surface. "That would ruin it. The fading paint jobs is one of the things that make it beautiful. All that history. Someone hand made this." She crouched down and looked up, making it clear that he needed to lean over too. When he did, she pointed out the underside of the top shelf. "Look at these joints. This was made by hand. And then repainted at least four times, one layer over top the next. And look at this."

He peered in at the bottom shelf she was indicating and noticed that there was the slightest indentation in the wood, as if a large book had been slid on and off the shelf, over and over and over again, enough to leave an impression in the wood.

"Whoever made this kept a Bible here." Vivian breathed.

"How do you know it was a Bible?"

"What else would it be? A book that size, one that they must have taken off the shelf nearly every day? So much that it would do this to the wood. Of course it was a Bible." She reached up toward him, and he helped her stand up again. "It makes me want to cry."

"Really?" He wasn't teasing her anymore. He genuinely wanted to know why a piece of furniture like this— as nice as it was—would affect her emotionally so much.

"I know you think I'm silly."

"No, I don't." He slid an arm around her waist, and she leaned against him in a deliciously trusting manner. "Tell me why it makes you cry."

"I don't know. Just the... the beauty of it, what it says about family and routine and faith and tradition. It's like a whole slice of human history represented by wood and paint and skill." She caressed the surface of the table again. "It's like Isaiah 60," she added.

He frowned, trying to remember the contents of that chapter. He knew his Bible well, having been raised in a Christian home, going to church and Sunday School all his life. But he didn't immediately recognize the reference. "What's that one?"

"It's that picture of the city of God in the future, in the new creation. All the peoples of the world offering their tribute, bringing what they have to God to help build his house. Camels and gold and cypress trees and..." Her voice drifted off for a moment. She was still staring at the table. "They bring the best that they have to him, and he accepts it. And then he uses it—what we bring—to beautify his beautiful house."

"Wow." Jeff breathed, after a moment of silence. It sounded like a pitiful understatement in response to what she'd just said, to how it had hit him, but she seemed to understand that he wasn't belittling it. She leaned against him more fully, and he wrapped both arms around her.

"He doesn't need anything to make his house beautiful. He's perfect beauty in and of himself. And yet he takes our offerings, the works of our hands and our minds, and he'll make it part of the beauty of eternity. Like this table."

"I guess I could bring him my spreadsheets," Jeff murmured after a minute.

She chuckled and stretched up to kiss his jaw lightly. "Of course you can. That's the whole point of that chapter. All the different peoples of the world have something different to offer him. And all of it is blessed by him, used by him to make eternity beautiful." She paused, pulling back to study his face. "You know that includes your spreadsheets, right?"

He'd never—not once in his life—thought about his work in the world that way. He'd always believed he could make a difference, even a small one, in building God's kingdom, but he'd never seen what he did as having eternal significance.

Not like this.

He was strangely awed—by the truth of it and by Vivian, who put pieces together in her mind that way and could bring out truths he'd never seen before. He had no idea what to say in response to it.

It was almost a full minute that they stood there together, one of his arms still wrapped around her.

He felt closer to her in that moment than he'd ever felt to anyone in his life. As if they weren't just breathing the same air, thinking the same thoughts—but like they were living in the same heartbeat.

Then she finally said, "I don't always feel like what I do... matters, not as much as what the rest of my family does."

"I know you don't," he murmured. "And I'm always trying to tell you it does."

"I know you do." She looked up at him, her lips finally turning up in a little smile. "I guess that's why passages like that vision in Isaiah mean so much to me. And this little table. This idea that we're not just throwing our work away for nothing—to be forgotten the next day, the next year, or after we die. But that God can use it, whatever it is, to make eternity more beautiful."

He met her eyes, something shaking inside him, so much feeling that he couldn't possibly process it, much less articulate.

He couldn't say anything.

He didn't seem to need to.

After a long, held gaze, Vivian finally glanced away, clearing her throat. "Sorry. That's all the theological reflections for today. I don't know why I just got in a rambling mood like that."

"You can get in that mood with me anytime." He tilted her head up and then leaned forward to brush her lips with his. "That's what I'm here for."

"You're here for a lot more than that."

She meant it.

She saw him as a lot more than a sounding board and an organizer and implementer for all her ideas.

She saw him, valued him, as a person.

Maybe she even wanted him.

There was something here between them, something he'd never let himself acknowledge before.

And it was more than they liked to kiss each other or they were good at working together. They trusted each other, and what better foundation could there be for a romantic relationship.

Maybe they could actually build a future together. It was early but not as early as it seemed since they'd known each other for so long.

Jeff wasn't going to run away from it, shy away from it, hide because it frightened him to risk his heart again.

This was more than worth the risk.

~

When they returned to Balm in Gilead an hour later, they were both unusually quiet. It didn't feel awkward though. It felt... intimate.

It was a new feeling between them, and one that Jeff just loved.

They didn't run into any of the other staff members as they walked into the building and then upstairs.

Jeff wanted to hold Vivian's hand, but he was afraid she would pull hers away. She'd said she didn't want their relationship to be made public yet, and it wouldn't be fair to force her into it without having a discussion.

He wanted to though. Have a discussion with her about their relationship.

He'd lived too long assuming a woman was committed to him, only to find out that she wasn't in the most painful of ways.

His heart was at stake, and all he wanted was for it to feel secure.

They made it to the third floor, stopping in front of Vivian's door.

She unlocked it and then turned back toward him. "I had... a really good time this afternoon," she murmured, dropping her eyes almost shyly.

His heart immediately jumped into a full-fledged rampage in his chest. "Me too," he said thickly.

The chime for the elevator sounded down the hall, and Vivian's eyes shot over to it. Responding to her obvious anxiety about someone seeing them, he stepped her backward into her room and closed the door behind them.

Then, because her body felt so good against his, he eased her back against the wall to the entryway.

She stared up at him, her eyes wide and excited and her cheeks turning pinker than before. "What do you think you're doing?" she asked breathlessly, a delicious lilt to her voice.

"Kissing you."

He'd always understood himself as being a man of his word, so he followed through on his words now. He leaned forward, catching her lips with his and then sliding his tongue out to tease them a little.

She made a little sound that went right to his groin as she pressed herself against him and slid her hands up to his shoulders. Her lips parted, and she gave herself over to the embrace with a passion, an eagerness, that only fueled his desire.

When his arousal grew too insistent, he forced himself to pull back, unable to stop himself from groaning softly at the difficulty of such self-restraint.

"You're quite a kisser, you know," she said, smiling up at him. She looked flushed and rumpled and pleased but not nearly as physically tortured as he was.

He chuckled. "Does that surprise you?"

"No. Not really. You're good at a lot of things." She paused for a moment, moving her hand up to caress his face, cheek, and jaw very gently. "You're good with me."

"I'm glad you think so. I plan to be good with you for as long as you'll let me."

The words came out as more intentional than he'd thought they would, and he saw their significance register in her eyes.

Before he could get worried about it though, she smiled up at him again. "Are you sure you want the responsibility? I'm not an easy woman, you know."

Her tone had been light, almost teasing, but Jeff frowned anyway. "What does that mean?"

"You know me, Jeff. I'm kind of... complicated. High maintenance. Guys don't usually like high maintenance. At least I assume that's why no one has ever wanted to be with me for very long."

"I like high maintenance. I like complicated. You're not going to scare me away, Vivian. I'm more than up for the challenge."

He'd obviously said the right thing—the thing she'd wanted to hear—because her face bloomed with pleasure, joy, something akin to awe.

It took Jeff's breath away.

He leaned down to kiss her again, very softly despite the continued compulsion of his groin. "I'm crazy about you, Vivian," he murmured against her mouth. "Exactly as you are."

It would have been nice if she'd said it back to him, but the way she wrapped her arms around him in a tight, emotional hug was response enough for him.

At least for now.

SEVEN

Vivian went to bed that night thinking about Jeff, and she woke up thinking about him still.

She had no idea what had happened, but the past four days had flipped some kind of switch in her mind, and now her whole being seemed to be focused on him—what he was thinking, what he was doing, what he was feeling about her, how he looked as he sipped his coffee over breakfast and occasionally slanted looks over her.

He was cute. Adorable. She'd always thought so. But now he was more than that. The chiseled line of his jaw, the strong curve of his shoulders under his golf shirt, the kink at the front of his thick hair he could never quite tame, the course hair on his forearms. Every detail she noticed. Every detail made him more attractive.

Every detail made her shiver in excitement.

It was honestly rather unnerving, after knowing Jeff for so long.

Even her memories of the serious, slightly geeky college guy had transformed, and she kept playing over the first few times she'd met him, wondering if there were any signs even back then that she'd one day feel for him this way.

She had to struggle to maintain her normal, confident demeanor over breakfast since she felt ridiculously like giggling and swooning over Jeff. But she'd worked hard to become the person she was, to have people look at her and see success and authority, and she wasn't going to throw all that away by acting like a high school girl over a cute guy.

She liked what was happening with Jeff. After their conversation in the primitives shop yesterday and then in her room afterward, she felt closer to him than ever, closer to him than she'd ever felt to another living person. She wanted it to continue, but she didn't want the entire world to know.

She wasn't even sure why.

It just made her feel... vulnerable. Like making it public would increase the odds of her getting hurt by this. So she wanted to keep it just between them.

Her social life wasn't the rest of the staff's business anyway.

"Oh, Viv," Rachel said just then, her green eyes sparkling behind her wire-framed glasses. "I've decided on the perfect guy for you."

Vivian stared, momentarily bewildered because it was like Rachel had literally read her mind.

The rest of the table grew silent in interest, and Vivian could feel Jeff's gaze moving from Rachel to Vivian. He was listening. She couldn't help but wonder what he was thinking.

Pleased that her cheeks weren't flushing too much from the wave of self-consciousness, Vivian manage to smile lightly. "Oh yeah? Who's that?"

With a mischievous smile lurking at the corners of her mouth, Rachel nodded across the large dining room.

Vivian turned automatically, and her eyes widened when she saw Zeke standing in the far corner, talking to Cecily. Today he wore a camouflage T-shirt and a pair of bright blue shorts—with orange deck sandals. His dark hair was standing on end, and his beard had clearly not been trimmed in weeks.

Rachel was visibly trying not to giggle. "What do you think?"

Vivian rolled her eyes. "Perfect," she said dryly. "It was like we were made for each other."

"Now, don't dismiss him out of hand. He's a really smart guy. He has a degree in mechanical engineering, and then he went to seminary for a year, although he never got a degree there. His wife died, and he dropped out."

Genuinely interested in this information, Vivian asked, "How do you know all that? Did you manage to get him to talk?"

"Of course not. He doesn't do anything more than growl when I ask him questions, but I asked around about him from other people who work here, and they told me. His wife died a while back, and that was when he let everything go. He dropped out of seminary and moved out here to work for Cecily. But I'm sure all he needs is a good woman to get him back on the right track. And maybe give him a good makeover." Rachel was smiling brightly. "You're just the person for the job."

"Uh-huh." Vivian was actually relieved by the turn of this conversation. Since Zeke was obviously not a real possibility for her, she didn't have to sidestep the topic without letting the others know she already had a man she was interested in. "Sounds perfect."

"I'm serious," Rachel protested. "You should try to talk to him. You never know! What if he's perfect for you?"

"That would be… unexpected," she said carefully, ensuring her tone was light and teasing. "But I suppose anything is possible. I'm sure he's a very nice guy under all the scowling."

"So you're going to try talking to him?" Rachel asked.

Vivian wished the topic had never come up, and she wished Jeff wasn't looking at her in that particular way, as if he was expecting something from her.

Did he expect her to announce to the table that she was actually already in a relationship with Jeff?

Surely not. They'd agreed to keep it secret for now.

"We'll see," she said with another smile, this one slightly more forced. "I'll see if the spirit moves me."

She couldn't resist shooting a glance over to Jeff, and their eyes met for a minute. He looked slightly amused, as if he understood how she was put on the spot, but also something else.

Maybe resignation.

Maybe disappointment.

Was he disappointed in her?

What had he wanted her to do?

How had she let him down?

She hated that feeling more than anything, and she brooded over it for the rest of breakfast, going back over what had been said and what she could have said differently.

She hated the idea that she might have let Jeff down, that she wasn't who he'd wanted her to be.

They were finished with breakfast when Cecily walked over to their table. Today she was wearing a pale gray pencil skirt and a vintage satin blouse, with heels that had a cute little buckle strap. Vivian eyed the outfit appreciatively, wishing she could pull off that look herself.

If she wore it though, she would look like she was wearing a costume.

"There's a phone call for you," Cecily said with a smile, her blue eyes focused on Vivian. "You can take it in the front office or in the sitting room off the lobby. Just press line three."

"Oh," Vivian said, surprised and starting to stand. "I wonder who it is."

"Your parents," Cecily replied. "It's no emergency, they said. They just wanted to say hi."

Vivian nodded, relieved after an immediate sharp pang of concern. There was no reason to expect an emergency, but they were out of the country and didn't always play it safe. She told the others she'd be back and walked into the lobby and then toward the sitting room, thinking that would be more private than the front office.

She sat for a few seconds, breathing deeply and putting on her game face before she picked up the phone.

As she did so, she had a sudden vision of Jeff, telling her she didn't need her game face.

Maybe that was true.

Maybe he was right.

She'd been completely herself with him for the past few days, and she was happier and more excited than she could ever remember being.

Maybe Jeff had a point.

"Good morning," she said brightly, after picking up the phone.

"Hello, dear," her mother said through a slightly crackly line. "Your father is here too. We were just thinking of you and wanted to see how you were doing."

Vivian couldn't help but smile. Who didn't want to hear that? "I'm doing good. Really good. How's the clinic going?"

"It's been a real success. We've been able to treat almost five hundred people. When we have more time, I have to tell you about this little girl I met, but I know you're on that retreat thing this week, so I don't want to take too much of your time."

"I have time," Vivian said. She paused to see if her mother would continue, tell her the story, but she didn't. If her mother got it in her head that it wasn't a good time, nothing she could say would convince her otherwise. "Well, be sure to tell me later," she added. "I'd love to hear about her."

"Of course, dear. How is the retreat going?"

"It's going really well. This is a great place, and everyone seems to be really enjoying it and unwinding."

"But not you, right?" Her mother's voice was teasing.

Vivian paused a moment. "I'm doing okay. I haven't used my phone in three days."

"Wow! Is that a record for you?"

"I think so. Since college anyway." She paused again, working on restoring her game face so she wouldn't sound anything but optimistic with her mother.

Then suddenly she imagined Jeff's eyes on her, understanding but also slightly disappointed.

He didn't think she needed to wear her game face all the time.

He thought she should be herself.

"And is there anything else happening with you?" her mother asked.

"Well, uh…" Vivian normally wouldn't have said a word to her parents about Jeff—not this early, not when things were this tenuous. But she had the sudden urge to be genuine, to be real, to try to really connect with her family.

They loved her, after all. They would be happy for her.

"There's something?" her mother prompted. "What on earth could it be?"

Vivian cleared her throat. "Well, uh, there might be... might be a man."

There was a pause on the other end, longer than normal.

Then, "Who?" The brief question was from her father.

Swallowing hard, Vivian admitted, "Jeff."

"Jeff?" her mother repeated.

"Yes, Jeff. Jeff Owen. My business partner. Remember him? You've met him before."

"Yes, of course we remember Jeff. So the two of you are courting now?"

Courting.

Right.

That was what they were doing.

Vivian cleared her throat again. "I don't know about courting. But we're... there might be something between us. It's just beginning, but... I don't know."

"That's very nice, dear," her mother said, sounding less surprised now. "Of course, I'll believe it's serious when it happens."

Vivian was feeling ridiculously nervous about admitting a truth this vulnerable to her parents, and now her mother's light tone felt like a slap. "Why wouldn't it be serious?"

"How many boyfriends have you had over the past ten years? How many of them were serious?"

"Some of them... I mean, I wasn't just playing around. The relationships just didn't work out."

"I know, dear. That happens, of course. You've always been so independent. Not everyone is made for marriage. There's so much more work you can do when you're single anyway. It's nothing to worry about."

Vivian realized—even through a blur of pain—that her mother was trying to be nice, trying to make her feel better, trying to assure her that she didn't need to be married to have value.

But even knowing this, it felt like an attack—like her parents had decided long ago that she was never going to get married, that she wasn't the kind of woman a man would want that way.

All the guys she'd dated in her life—from her high school boyfriend to that attorney a year and a half ago—had all obviously come to the same conclusion.

There was something about her—underneath the surface—that men just didn't want.

Her throat hurt so much she couldn't immediately respond.

Maybe her mother picked up something in the quality of the silence because her tone was softer when she continued, "But if this is the real thing with Jeff, then of course we're happy for you."

"I... I don't know if it's the real thing or not."

It felt different—being with Jeff. It felt different than it had felt with any other man in her entire life.

But that didn't necessarily mean it was real.

It didn't necessarily mean that Jeff would always want her.

"Then just give yourself time to figure it out. He always struck me as a very thoughtful, intelligent young man. He's not going to want to jump into anything anyway."

That was very possibly true.

Jeff was smart. And he was thoughtful. And he usually made good decisions.

He might return home after the week was over and realize he'd made a huge mistake in kissing her for the first time.

"Are you upset, dear?" her mother asked after another moment's pause. "I didn't mean to upset you."

Vivian took a breath. Put back on her game face. With a smile she knew could be heard in her voice, she said, "Of course not. It's just... this thing with him is new, and I don't know what to make of it yet."

"Then you'll figure it out."

They chatted for another minute, and then Vivian hung up the phone.

She slumped forward, dropping her head in her hands for a minute—suddenly feeling heavy, exhausted, helpless.

Like nothing she could do would ever be enough.

Then she straightened up and squared her shoulders. She glanced in a wall mirror as she got up to leave the room.

She looked fresh and natural today—with no makeup except mascara and undone hair. But it was still a basically pretty face, and her lavender top was cute and flattering.

She was still Vivian Harper. She was who she'd always been.

And she could always show the world her best face.

Willing her roiling feelings back down to a dark corner of her heart, she walked out of the sitting room and into the lobby.

The first person she saw was Zeke.

He appeared to be repairing a broken leg on a console table against the wall.

"What happened to it?" Vivian asked, coming over to stand beside it.

Zeke looked up, his blue eyes visibly surprised above his dark messy beard. "Broke," he grunted.

She gave a huff of laugher. "Obviously. I was just wondering how it got broken. Is it some sort of secret?"

Zeke's eyes searched her face, and his scowl lessened slightly. "It got knocked over by a suitcase."

She could well imagine the scene. Some poor hapless guest let their suitcase roll at the wrong angle, very likely suffering the wrath of Zeke's scowl at the damage to part of what he considered his responsibility. "Too bad," she murmured, her lip twitching slightly.

Zeke was still eyeing her, almost suspiciously, as he stood up. "What's going on?"

"What do you mean?"

He glanced around the otherwise empty lobby. "Did someone put you up to this?"

This was the most she'd heard him speak—ever. In a way, it was a kind of victory. "Of course not. Can't someone just have a conversation with you without an underlying motive?"

"Not really," he muttered. He was looking at her for real though. Still peering at her, trying to figure her out.

"Well, I don't have a motive. I just find you interesting." She smiled at him. It was a good smile. It usually got a very good response from men.

Zeke shook his head. "No, you don't."

"Yes, I do!" He was definitely the strangest man she'd ever met. She pitied Cecily, for having to put up with him on a daily basis. "Don't you ever smile?"

"Sure."

"When?"

Zeke's eyes left hers, shifting over to somewhere past her shoulder.

Vivian turned to look and saw Cecily standing in the doorway to her office, talking to Jeff.

Both Jeff and Cecily were watching them.

Vivian met Jeff's eyes and was hit with the strangest feeling.

Guilt.

Like she'd done more than disappointed him. Like she'd somehow betrayed him.

All she was doing was talking to Zeke. She wasn't even really flirting with him. She was just being friendly. She was allowed to do that. She could talk to anyone she wanted.

But Jeff's brown eyes were sober, knowing, as they rested on her.

Vivian had to turn away from what she saw there.

"When?" she asked again, focusing on Zeke again. "When do you smile?"

Zeke's attention turned back to her too. "When there's reason," he muttered. Then he knelt back down to continue working on the table.

Vivian was about to walk over to Jeff, feeling kind of sick all of a sudden and wanting to get rid of the feeling. Wanting to fix things. But the rest of the staff had appeared in the lobby from the dining room, and they surrounded her.

By the time she'd finished talking to them, Jeff was already gone.

~

Vivian struggled for about a half hour, trying to figure out if she really had any reason to feel guilty.

She decided she did.

It wasn't wrong to be friendly with Zeke.

She knew it wasn't.

But still…

She'd been doing it for a reason, and that reason wasn't worthy.

Finally she felt so bad that she had to do something to fix it. She went upstairs and knocked on Jeff's door.

She didn't even know if he was there, but she didn't know where else to look for him.

He opened the door after a minute. He didn't say anything, and he didn't smile, although he didn't look angry or resentful.

Just quiet.

And really tired.

"I'm sorry!" she blurted out.

"For what?"

It was a test. She knew it was, and she didn't begrudge it. He wanted to know if she understood what was bothering him.

So she told him. "I was… upset. I was trying to feel better. I wasn't being… real. I shouldn't have flirted with him. But you know I'm not interested in Zeke, right?"

"I know," Jeff said softly. "What happened with your parents?"

She shook her head, not wanting to go into it, not wanting to cry, which she was afraid she might do if she talked about it.

He waited a moment, still standing in the doorway to his room. "You're not going to tell me?"

She glanced down the hall. "Can I at least come in?"

Jeff's face relaxed slightly. "Of course. Sorry."

She stepped inside, and he closed the door behind her.

It was strange being in his room. A pair of shoes was on the floor next to the bed. A shirt and a pair of shorts were draped over a chair. There was a book lying on the covers and a half-drunk bottle of water on the nightstand.

It felt... intimate.

"You want to sit?" Jeff asked, gesturing toward the chairs by the window. "Or we can sit on the balcony."

"Let's go to the balcony." The sun was warm but not oppressive today, and for some reason outside felt safer to her.

They went outside, and she sat down on one of the straight chairs at the table. Jeff sat on the chaise.

"What happened with your parents?" he asked again.

"Nothing really. We just talked."

"Why do you try to foist me off like that? You were okay this morning, but then you talked to your parents, and now you're... damaged, fragile. Tell me what happened."

His voice had taken on that tone that brooked no argument, and his expression had changed to his stubborn face.

"It really wasn't anything," she admitted, resting her head on one hand propped on the table. "They just... I tried to tell them about us, and they didn't think it could be serious. They don't think anyone is ever going to want to marry me."

He was searching her face, and she saw several expressions flicker across his own before he said, "Why not?"

She shrugged. "I'm too independent or something. It's silly to be upset about it. I wish... I wish I hadn't even told them."

"You should be able to tell them the truth."

"I know. I wanted to... but... I don't know what's wrong with me. I have no idea why I'm so upset about it."

"They're your parents. Of course they have the power to hurt you."

"But they're not bad parents. They're never mean or selfish or... They're not bad parents."

"I know they're not. And I'm sure they love you and are trying to do what's best. But they've always made you feel like you're not good enough, and they're still doing it today."

"They're not—"

"Yes, they are. And you believe them more than you believe me."

She stared at him, so surprised she couldn't immediately respond. "What do you mean?"

"I mean you believe them when they make you think you're not good enough. You don't believe me when I say you are."

"I do believe you. I know I have no reason to feel bad about myself. I *know* it."

"You just don't always believe it."

She sat for a minute, staring blindly at the floor.

Jeff didn't say anything either.

She was shaking slightly, but she didn't want to cry. It felt like she'd cried enough this week.

She wasn't normally like this.

She'd never thought of herself as an insecure person. It made no sense that it was all coming out this week.

"Come here, honey," Jeff murmured after a full minute of silence.

She glanced up at him in surprise.

He'd lifted a hand to gesture her toward him, and his face was very soft, warm, tender.

Her throat ached as she got up and went to him. There was no way she could resist.

He pulled her down in the chaise with him, her body stretched out against his. He wrapped both his arms around her and pressed a few kisses against her hair.

His touch was so gentle that she started to shake even harder, emotion rippling through her.

He tightened his arms around her as she buried her face in his chest.

He didn't say anything. He didn't have to. She could feel his support, his acceptance, his complete understanding in every inch of his body pressed against hers.

He cared about her. Exactly as she was. Even falling apart for no reason this way.

He didn't care if she was falling apart. He still wanted to hold her, to be beside her. She'd never really believed it was possible.

But there was no way she could doubt it or question it.

This was what it felt like to be with someone for real.

She'd never really understood it before.

~

The lay together on the chaise for a long time, not talking, just holding each other.

When the emotion finally relaxed inside her, she pulled away from him just enough to look up at his face.

His expression was quiet. And tender in a way that made her heart jump.

It still didn't seem like it could be real—that a man, that Jeff, was looking at her like that, like she was the most important thing in his world.

"I'm really sorry," she said, her voice cracking from her earlier emotion and from what she was feeling right now.

"You don't have to say it again," Jeff murmured, stroking her hair back from her face.

"I know. But I want to. I feel bad about it. I want to fix it."

"See, and I don't want you to try to fix it. That's what you do when you're trying to be perfect, trying to put on that perfect, pretty face for the world. I don't want that from you. All I want is for you to be real with me. *Real*. With *me*."

He was utterly serious. She heard it in his voice. Saw it in his eyes.

And she understood it.

She wanted it too.

She might not have ever experienced it before, but she had with him this week. And she wanted it. More of it. More than anything.

"Okay," she said, resting her head against his shoulder. "If real is what you want, then real is what you'll get."

She felt him let his breath out in a long sigh. "Good. That's all I want. Just be real with me. Tell me the truth. Don't always try to protect yourself. Trust me not to hurt you."

She couldn't help but laugh softly. "That's a pretty ambitious request, you know."

"I've always been an ambitious guy." He brushed a kiss into her hair. "But that's the deal with us. That's what I want."

She adjusted so she could kiss his lips. "That's what I want too."

She meant it.

She'd never meant it before—not with any of the men she'd ever gone out with—but she meant it with Jeff.

EIGHT

The morning Kaylee had walked out on Jeff, he'd woken up hopeful and optimistic.

They'd been fighting for weeks, and he'd been alternating between despair and simmering frustration, but he'd made the resolution to really try to work things out again. He'd planned a romantic dinner and had even bought her a gift—an expensive pair of earrings—so she would know he wasn't trying to keep nice things from her just because.

He'd gone over the evening again and again in his mind throughout the day, and he was excited as he got home.

He'd found a mostly empty apartment.

Kaylee had taken almost everything—including a couple of pieces of furniture he'd owned before they got married.

He still felt nauseated when he remembered that moment—the empty apartment, a concrete symbol of exactly what she'd wanted from him.

And how little she'd wanted *him*.

He felt a flicker of that same feeling as he opened his eyes in Balm in Gilead on his last full day there. Nothing really prompted it. He could just feel it roiling in his gut.

It was just natural, he supposed, to think about this past relationship when he was building a new one.

And he *was* building a new one. There was no question about that. He and Vivian had come to some sort of crossroads the day before. Both of them knew it. She'd let go

118

of what she'd been holding on to; she'd surrendered the social mask she liked to wear.

They'd been together for real as they lay together on the balcony yesterday, and he'd known she knew it too.

He was in love with her.

No sense in trying to deny it.

He'd probably loved her for a while now but had been trying not to recognize it.

He could now.

She was in this too.

His heart could be safe with her.

They'd come to a resolution yesterday afternoon, and both of them knew it.

He wasn't going to make another mistake like he did with Kaylee.

Tomorrow they'd be going back home, back to the normal world. But things wouldn't be the same as they'd been before.

He'd have Vivian now.

He pushed down the faint sick feeling, prompted by a two-year-old memory, as he lay in bed and stared up at the ceiling.

Soon he felt hopeful and optimistic.

Something good was going to happen today. He wasn't going to run away from it either.

He was going make sure it happened.

Both he and Vivian were over thirty. There was no reason to play around or waste time. If they wanted to be in a relationship, then they should really do it. She'd hesitated at first, but that had changed yesterday. She was in this as much as he was now.

He spent a few minutes—not getting out of bed—imagining what it would be like to date Vivian, to get engaged to her, to marry her, to make love to her, maybe even to have children.

The imaginings were so irresistible to him that he could have stayed in bed thinking them through for much longer. But he was usually up and dressed by now, and he didn't want Vivian to knock on his door and discover him still in bed.

So he rolled out of bed and took a quick shower. He was pulling on a shirt when there was a knock on the door.

He swung it open to find Vivian standing there, wearing shorts and a sleeveless top that showed off her shapely arms and legs and tanned skin. She was giving him an intimate little smile.

His heart leapt in his chest, and he smiled like a dope back at her.

"Did you sleep in?" she asked, her blue eyes taking in his damp hair and lack of shoes.

"A little."

"You didn't even shave." She lifted a hand to rub her palm along his jaw. The light touch was delicious against his stubble, and he had to smother a moan.

"Maybe I'll grow a beard," he managed to say in a dry voice.

She chuckled. "I don't know if you're the beard kind."

"I could be the beard kind."

Her eyes were soft and amused. "If you grow a beard, you'll have to stop always wearing ties to work."

"Is there some rule against tie wearing and beard growing?"

"Of course there's a rule. It's one of the foundational rules of the universe. Guys who grow beards can't always wear ties to work."

He tried to think of something smart to say to sustain their banter, but he couldn't do it. His heart was too full of her—of this clever, funny, beautiful, generous woman—and there was nothing he could do but respond to the feeling.

He pulled her into a hug.

She hugged him back, and he held her in his arms for a moment in the entrance of his bedroom.

It would be nice—really nice—if he could pull her into his room all the way, carry her to his bed, show her exactly how much he loved her, body and heart.

But it wasn't their time yet, so he pushed down the urge enough to loosen his arms.

She was flushed and smiling as she pulled away. "You're in quite a mood today."

"I woke up thinking about you," he told her.

"Me too," she admitted. "I woke up thinking about you too."

~

They went down to breakfast, and then the staff went to the craft room at Mel's suggestion so they could make another scrapbook of memories and compare their impressions and creative abilities between the first day and today.

Jeff didn't actually like crafting of any kind—not any more than he had when he'd first arrived—but he had a good time anyway, watching the staff interact in an easy, friendly, relaxed manner and watching Vivian in particular.

Everyone seemed to have a good time here this week.

Everyone looked more rested and refreshed and genuine.

And Vivian in particular. She'd shed that perfect mask she always wore and was really being herself. She was having a good time, but it was more than that.

She wasn't trying to make sure everyone liked and respected her. She was here for real, happy for real.

And he couldn't help the swell of pride that he was part of the reason it was true.

She needed him. He could really help her. He had something to offer her that she recognized, appreciated, valued.

He wasn't just a date or a business partner to her.

She wanted him for who he really was.

By the end of the morning, he was more determined than ever to make this evening really special, think of some way of capping their week with a night she'd never forget.

He had no idea how to do it though. He was limited to the resources of the center, and he wasn't even sure what those resources were.

After lunch, he went to find Zeke. He needed to ask someone who worked here, and no matter how taciturn and unsmiling Zeke was, Jeff was more comfortable asking him than Cecily with her characteristic prim coolness.

He wandered around for a few minutes and found Zeke outside, working on the flower beds that ran along the sides of the pool deck.

"Hey," he said, trying to sound casual. It wasn't a normal tone for him, so he wasn't sure he succeeded. "I was wondering if you could help me with something."

Zeke looked up from where he was crouching on the ground. He didn't say anything, but he was obviously waiting and listening.

Jeff cleared his throat, feeling like an idiot. "I was wanting to... to do something special this evening... for someone." Damn, could he manage to sound any stupider? "But I wasn't sure what was possible. Here. I mean, I wasn't sure what you had here I could use."

Zeke blinked. "Special?" he asked gruffly.

"Romantic," Jeff admitted.

He was normally a mature, basically confident man. Only Vivian could make him willing to feel like such a fool.

Zeke didn't reply for a moment, and his face reflected no expression. Then he said curtly, "We have a boat."

Jeff raised his eyebrows. "What?"

"We have a boat," Zeke repeated.

It took a few seconds for Jeff to process, but he eventually realized the words weren't just a random, disconnected statement. Zeke was actually making a suggestion for something he might do for a romantic evening.

Jeff relaxed slightly. "Oh. Yeah. That might be good. She'd enjoy that. Although I'm not much of a boater."

"Just a small motorboat. It's easy to handle. I can show you."

"Okay. That would be great. Thanks."

"You should get a bottle of wine," a new voice came from behind Jeff.

He turned to see Daniel Duncan, leaning against the railing with an amused smile.

"Sorry," Daniel added. "I couldn't help but overhear. But you should definitely get a bottle of wine. And finger food. Something easy to eat. Don't try something that needs plates or forks. I've tried that for a romantic picnic, and it ended up being a huge pain. And a mess."

Jeff chuckled, not even offended by this intrusion. "Yeah. I don't think I'm going to try a four-course meal on a boat. But wine and finger food is a good idea."

"There's a market in Buxton," Zeke said, still not smiling although he seemed genuinely engaged in the conversation. "They have flowers too."

Flowers. He could get Vivian flowers.

"Okay. Great. When can you help me with the boat."

"Hour or two. Just come find me."

Jeff nodded and thanked the man, who soon apparently forgot he existed.

Daniel was still standing nearby, an amused look in his eyes. "Easy food and nothing messy," he said. "That's my best suggestion."

"Got it. So you've made a mess of a romantic evening before?"

"More than once," Daniel said. "Although my wife almost burned the house down in her attempt to create a romantic evening for us once, so I still say I've come out ahead."

Jeff laughed. He genuinely liked this man, and he wasn't embarrassed about someone else knowing his plans.

He was excited now about tonight.

He wanted to tell Vivian that he loved her, and he wasn't even afraid.

~

The romantic evening didn't go quite as smoothly as he had hoped.

He went to the store to buy what he needed, and then he found Zeke, who showed him the boat and how to use it.

It wasn't very large. It wasn't very complicated. Jeff wasn't worried about making it move or getting it out onto the water where he wanted to.

But the first complication came when he discovered Vivian had made other plans for the evening. She and the staff were going to sit around the fire pit on the beach one last time before they left. Vivian looked happy, pleased with the idea, and Jeff had no idea how to convince her that he had a better idea.

As he stood still in the hallway, trying to think of some way to handle this, Vivian frowned and stepped closer to him.

"What's the matter?" she asked, searching his face with something between confusion and concern.

"Nothing."

"Well, something's wrong. You sound like you don't want to join us this evening. You don't have to if you don't want, but everyone would think it was strange. Aren't you feeling good?"

Her eyes were soft on his face, and in any other situation, he would love the tender intimacy of her look, as if she had every right to take care of him, to find out what he wasn't saying.

Now, however, it was very inconvenient. "I feel fine."

"Then what's the matter? Are you feeling antisocial for some reason? You haven't been around much all afternoon. I looked for you."

"I was… busy. I'm not feeling antisocial." She wasn't going to let it go, and there was no possible excuse for his response, so he had no choice but to tell her the truth. "I was just… I thought we might do something else this evening."

"Like what?" She still had absolutely no idea. Her eyes were wide and innocent. "I'm sure the others would be willing to do something else if—"

"Not the others. Just us." For no good reason he felt silly explaining himself. And really young.

Her eyes widened even more, and her lips parted slightly. He saw the recognition wash over her face.

"It's not really a big deal," he said. "I just thought maybe you and I could…"

"Do something else," she finished for him, her mouth turning up just slightly in a little smile.

"Yes."

Her smile widened, and she leaned forward, kissing him gently, deliciously. "You're the sweetest man. Did you know that?"

He rolled his eyes at her. "You can mock if you want."

"I wasn't mocking! You really are sweet. There aren't many guys left like you around anymore."

Since she seemed to mean it, despite the soft amusement in her tone, he relaxed and slipped his arms around her waist. "Then you better hold on to the one you have."

"You don't have to tell me that. I already know." She kissed him again, just as lightly as before. Then she asked, "What did you have planned for tonight?"

"What does it matter if we aren't going to be able to do it?"

"Maybe we still can. We can do the beach thing with the others but call it an early evening. Say we're tired or whatever. Would we still have time afterward?"

"Sure," he said, his heart warming at the realization that she wanted them to do what he'd planned, that she wanted to spend the evening with him even if they had to do some maneuvering to make it work.

It was like a miracle. Like a dream.

That Vivian—his Vivian Harper—wanted to be with him like that.

"Good," she said. "We'll do it afterward then. I'm looking forward to it."

So was he.

~

So after that first complication was dealt with, things went fine for a while. They had an early dinner with the others—after Vivian had declared she was starving and they needed to eat early tonight—and then they went down to the beach to sit around the fire pit. Garrett brought his guitar again, and they hung out for more than an hour.

At a quarter to eight, however, Jeff was starting to get restless. He wanted to move on to the next part of the evening, and the others showed no signs of wrapping up. Vivian kept meeting his eyes, and he could see she was amused by his impatience.

She might want to spend the evening with him, but she wasn't in a hurry—not like he was.

He hemmed and hawed for about ten minutes, trying to find a time to break in and declare it time to call it a night. Every time he started to speak, though, someone else would beat him to it, suggesting another song or telling another story.

Eventually, Jeff felt like groaning every time anyone opened their mouth.

Finally Vivian must have taken pity on him. She stretched her arms over her head and yawned loudly. "All right. You all can stay out here longer if you want, but I'm going to call it quits for the night."

If the others were surprised by her early retreat, they didn't act that way. The others followed her lead—as they nearly always did—and everyone agreed to break up the group for the evening.

As everyone wandered off in different directions, Jeff lingered on the beach, waiting with Vivian until the others were out of sight.

No one would think it was strange. He and Vivian talked privately all the time, and it would be normal for them to walk back together.

When they were finally alone, he took her hand and led her down the beach toward the boat dock.

"Where are we going?" Vivian asked, having to walk quickly to keep up with his stride.

"You'll see."

"I thought your head was going to explode for a few minutes there."

"You could have helped me out earlier, you know."

"I know. But it was just too funny watching you bite back your annoyance every time someone said something."

"I've planned a very romantic evening here," he told her with narrowed eyes. "You could try to be a little appreciative, you know."

"I do appreciate it." Her face was flushed and warm and pretty and fond. "What kind of romantic evening do you have planned?"

"Just tell me you don't get seasick." It had never even occurred to him, but that would be the perfect ironic end to this day.

"What? No, of course not. Are we going out on a boat?"

"Yes."

He led her down the dock to where the small boat was tied. It was all prepared, thanks to Zeke, and Jeff had put all his provisions in earlier.

It was just after eight. The sun hadn't yet set. It was a warm, pleasant evening, and he was going out on a boat at sunset with Vivian.

He didn't even mind the slight frustrations in getting to this place.

"Oh, it's perfect," Vivian said as she situated herself in the boat and saw the wine and bag of groceries and flowers he'd gotten. "I can't believe you did all this."

The humor had left her face now. She looked almost awed. And very touched.

Jeff's heart did a familiar little flip-flop. "Why wouldn't I do it?"

"For me?" she breathed.

She was such a complex incongruity of confidence and insecurity—always so polished and sure of herself, except when it went deep. He reached out and cupped her cheek with one hand. "Only for you," he murmured, rather thickly.

Fortunately, the complications he'd faced in getting here disappeared as soon as they set off from the dock. The boat moved easily, and he had no trouble steering or turning it. They went out far enough so it felt like they were completely alone, and they drank wine and ate bread and cheese and grapes and strawberries and chocolate truffles as the sun set.

Eventually the food and wine were gone, and it was starting to get dark. Vivian was leaning against him, and his arm was holding her close. Everything felt just about perfect, and he knew she felt the same way.

It felt like it had the previous day when they'd been lying on the chaise together on his balcony.

But better.

Even better.

This was the moment—the moment when he could finally know for sure his heart was safe.

She wasn't going to hurt him, reject him, throw him away the way Kaylee did.

They'd agreed to be real with each other, and he believed it was true.

She wanted this as much as he did.

She turned her head to gaze up at him, her eyes almost glazed with pleasure and something deeper. "Thank you for doing this," she murmured.

"You don't have to thank me. I wanted to."

"Well, I'm glad you wanted to, but it must have taken some work and planning, so I should be able to thank you for it anyway. I didn't even know you could drive a boat."

"I can't really. Zeke showed me how."

"You actually managed to get Zeke to help you? That was definitely an impressive feat."

"He actually was good about helping. I don't think he's a bad guy underneath all the rudeness."

"Maybe not. But I still appreciate everything you did. I'm never going to forget tonight."

"Good. Me either." He stroked her hair back from her face and then couldn't resist the lovely curve of her lips. He leaned forward to kiss her. "I love you, you know."

He'd wanted to tell her. All day he'd been thinking about telling her. But he hadn't really planned to say it then.

As soon as he said the words, he felt a chill of anxiety. Maybe he should have waited longer. Now he felt naked, vulnerable, uncertain—and he hated feeling that way.

She blinked, staring at him in the dim light from the boat and the moon and the stars. The sun was gone now, taking most of the light in the world with it.

She opened her mouth, but nothing came out. She closed it again and let out a little breath.

His heart, which had been bursting to near explosion for a while now, suddenly dropped painfully.

This wasn't good.

This couldn't be good.

"Jeff," she said at last.

He cleared his throat. "You can't be surprised, Vivian."

"I'm... I don't know. I mean, it means a lot to me— that you'd say that—but it's... it's still early. Too early for that."

He could see, in a certain way, that her words made perfect sense. They'd been together romantically for less than a week.

But they'd been together in every other way for years.

Despite the way this felt like a complete rejection, he was determined not to be unreasonable. Just because Kaylee had rejected him didn't mean Vivian would too.

He took a deep breath and nodded. "I understand. It hasn't been that long since things have changed. I know."

She was searching his face almost desperately, as if she was searching for signs of his feelings. "You're upset."

"Of course I'm upset," he said, still striving for calm despite the aching irony in his tone. "But I do understand. It's okay."

She swallowed visibly and inclined her head as if she realized how he felt and sympathized. "I'm really sorry. It's just... so soon."

He nodded again and said with more composure, "I know. As long as you're in this for real, I'm really okay."

"I am." She reached over to put a hand on his forearm. "I really am. I promise."

He could see on her face that she meant it, and he was able to take a deep breath for the first time. "Good. I'm glad."

She smiled, a slight sheen of tears in her eyes. "This is real, Jeff. I'm in it for real. I've never... It's never been like this for me before."

He took a deep breath and started to relax.

He could do this. He could be patient. He wasn't going to get his heart broken again.

Vivian wasn't Kaylee. History wasn't going to repeat itself.

He was safe in this. She might not be able to say the words.

"So it's okay if we at least let the staff know we're dating?" he asked, wanting final confirmation of his reflections.

He was watching her carefully, so he immediately saw when something froze up in her expression.

His heart sank, and this time no attempt at reasonableness could bring it back up.

He knew what this meant.

He *knew*.

"If this is real," he said slowly, "then surely we don't have to keep it private."

"It is real," Vivian said, growing urgent again. "But it's still so early—"

"It's not early. Maybe it's early for I love you, but it's not too early to treat this as something more than a dirty secret."

She gasped at his last words, as if he had struck her. "I don't think it's dirty, I just…"

"Don't want anyone to know you're with me."

"It's not about you. It's…" She couldn't seem to find the words to finish the thought.

He didn't need the words. He understood completely.

And the understanding had crashed down around him like a tidal wave.

He had to wait for a minute before he'd managed to compose himself. Then he finally said in an unnaturally calm voice, "I'm okay with you not being able to tell me you love me. But I'm not okay with this. You agreed that we would be real with each other. This isn't being real. This… isn't what I want."

Part of him ached at the fear flickering on her face as he spoke, like she knew she had just stepped over a cliff but there was no way to pull herself back. But the rest of him was feeling that same wash of absolute rejection he'd felt when Kaylee had cleared out their house and walked out on him without a word.

And there was no talking himself out of it this time.

"Don't say that, Jeff. Can't we just wait for a little while longer?"

"How long?"

She gave a helpless shrug.

"You don't know because you're not sure we're actually going to ever get to that point."

Vivian made a little wordless noise. Then she took a breath and said, "Please. Things are going well. Why do you have to—"

"Why do I have to what? Take this seriously? Take you seriously? You're saying I shouldn't?"

"Jeff, don't make it sound like that."

"Like what?"

"Like I don't care. You know I do care. You know how much this… this means to me."

He did know.

He'd seen her change over the past week, open up to him in a way she never had before, in a way she never had with anyone.

But he'd been wrong about her too.

He'd thought she was in this all the way, and she clearly wasn't—not like he was.

He'd thought he could trust her not to reject him, and he couldn't. Not really.

She was still looking for a way out—in case she wanted one later.

"It means a lot to you, but you don't want anyone to know about me," he said in that same clipped voice he didn't like. There was no other way he could speak though, not without completely losing it, completely humiliating himself.

"I'm not ashamed of you or anything, Jeff. I'm just not ready to… to…" She trailed off, and there was a little sob in her voice.

She was almost as upset as he was.

Almost.

For a moment he couldn't say anything.

Vivian swiped a tear away and reached out to clench his shirt in one of her hands. "Jeff, please don't do this. This doesn't feel right—for you to be angry at me because I'm not in exactly the same place you are."

"You think I'm angry?" he breathed.

She winced, as if she'd been stabbed. "Jeff, I'm doing the best I can. I told you that I was… I was complicated and high maintenance and wouldn't be an easy person to be with. I'm… I'm trying. You said you were up for the challenge."

He had said that, and he'd even meant it—but she could hardly expect him to keep pouring himself into something if she wasn't going to reciprocate, if she was going to keep holding back on him.

If she didn't really want him after all.

They sat together in silence for more than a minute, no sound except the soft slap of the water against the boat and their heavy breathing.

"Jeff?" she said at last, the one word an aching question.

"Let's go back," he said.

135

She grabbed at his arm. "Jeff, are you serious?"

"Yes, I'm serious. You're the one who isn't. You're the one who's just trying something out with me."

She gave a little jerk as if he'd struck a blow.

Then she clenched her jaw and gave a small nod. "Okay. Fine." She wasn't meeting his eyes, but she also wasn't crying anymore. "If that's the way it is, then fine."

Jeff felt sick. Physically ill. His stomach churned with it as he took them back to the dock.

Vivian got out of the boat quickly, even before he'd tied it up.

She looked like she was about to hurry away, but she glanced back at him once more before she did.

She didn't say anything, and it was dark, so her face wasn't clearly visible.

But it felt like her look was a question.

He shook his head, knowing the answer, realizing he should have known it all long, had he not let his foolish dreams and desires lead him astray again. "This isn't going to work," he said hoarsely.

"Okay," she said, sounding like she was swallowing the one word. "You're probably right."

She turned and walked away—striding quickly across the sand in the dark.

He should go with her. He shouldn't let her walk by herself on the beach at night. It was a private beach, but there was nothing to keep strangers out.

He stood where he was and watched her go.

He hadn't handled that well. At all. He'd reacted out of pain, and he'd hurt her in the process.

But ultimately it was for the best.

She'd taken this too well.

She hadn't been torn apart by what was clearly a breakup.

Her heart wasn't breaking like his was.

So whatever had been between them would have fallen apart eventually.

Better to do it now while he still had some hope of saving a few small pieces of his heart.

NINE

Vivian cried most of the night.

She must have fallen asleep at some point because she woke up as the sun started to stream in through her windows. She managed to open her eyelids, although the bright light hurt her aching eyes.

There was one moment of blurred enjoyment, when the world felt mostly like it should have felt. Then she remembered what had happened the evening before, and everything became raw and wrong and painful again.

She couldn't believe Jeff had dumped her, that he didn't want her enough to give her a little more space, make sure she was really ready for this relationship.

It was hard enough to process this, understand that Jeff had already given up on her.

But it was even harder to wonder if it was mostly her own fault.

Maybe she should have just told him she loved him too—even though the moment had been so terrifying that the words had strangled in her throat.

She'd felt it. Her heart last night had been as full as it had ever been.

But saying the words would have changed everything—about her, about her life, about the person she'd always been. Naturally, it was scary. It would have been scary for anyone.

If she couldn't say the words, she should have at least agreed to go public with their relationship.

She wasn't even sure why she'd resisted.

The resistance had been real and strong and overwhelming, but maybe she should have just pushed through so Jeff wouldn't have felt that kind of rejection.

She knew all about how rejection like that felt.

She was feeling it now, deeply, so much so that the grief and pain lodged in her gut like a rock.

Sometimes the thing that made you cry felt less big, less painful, when you woke up the following morning. And sometimes you were just too tired to cry.

Neither one of those things was true for Vivian at the moment. She lay in bed, blinking against the morning light, and she felt her eyes swelling up again, burning as all the emotion of the previous night came rising up again—into her heart, into her throat, into her eyes.

She blinked back the tears and made herself sit up.

She couldn't lie in bed and mope all day today. She wasn't at home. It was the end of her company retreat. She needed to get up, get dressed, go down to breakfast, put on her game face for the staff as they wrapped things up.

Maybe she could get a ride home with Mel. She wasn't sure she could face being alone in a car with Jeff for even a few hours.

But she could make it through the morning. Then she could go home and hibernate for the rest of the weekend. And on Monday morning she'd be feeling better. She could return to the office, act like her old self, make sure no one knew how painfully Jeff had broken her heart.

Eventually it wouldn't hurt like this.

Eventually she would feel better.

She prayed for a few minutes, staring up at the ceiling, asking for help, for strength, for God to somehow put her back together again.

She didn't feel any stronger afterward, but she had to get up anyway.

She showered. Dried her hair. Put on a cute, sleeveless top and a pair of blue-gray capris. When a few tears slipped out of her eyes as she was putting on her shoes, she had to go back to the bathroom mirror and fix her eye makeup.

She smiled at herself in the mirror.

It didn't look real to her, but maybe it would be convincing.

After all, people didn't usually look at others very carefully. Everyone was always absorbed in their own thoughts, their own issues.

She wondered what Jeff was thinking, feeling today.

When she finally concluded that she could make it through breakfast, she opened the door to her room and stepped out into the hallway.

It was empty.

There was no sound from Jeff's room next door.

She didn't knock on it as she normally would have. She just walked to the elevator and went down.

She ran into Rachel and Garrett in the lobby, and their cheerful greetings were a relief. She responded to them naturally, even managing to smile. She could do this. She could act normal.

She could make sure no one knew what had happened to her last night.

They were in the dining room, filling their breakfast plates at the bar, when Jeff came into the room. He must have been outside walking because there was a slight sheen of perspiration on his skin and his thick hair was windblown.

He was quiet, sober, strangely cool as he came over to join them and get a plate of his own. He shot Vivian one quick glance—as if he couldn't help himself—but then he avoided her eyes.

She knew because she kept watching him.

He wasn't looking at her.

He wasn't smiling.

He wasn't saying anything.

And it was all so completely wrong. As wrong as anything had ever been.

Rachel and Garrett—and the others when they trickled down from upstairs—didn't seem to notice anything was unusual about Jeff or Vivian. They all chatted cheerfully, going over their impressions about the center from the past week they'd spent and making plans for another retreat.

Everyone seemed to have had a great time.

Jeff had been right that the retreat was good for the staff.

It could have been good for Vivian, too, if her heart hadn't been ripped out of her chest on the last day.

She managed to respond mostly appropriately whenever someone brought her into the conversation, but Jeff didn't respond at all. Eventually the others seemed to notice his absolute silence.

When Grace asked him a direct question and he didn't even seem to hear her, Vivian saw Grace and Mel frowning at each other in confusion.

"Hey, Jeff," Garrett said, leaning over to try to catch the other man's eyes. "People are talking to you."

Jeff looked over, blinking as if he hadn't realized anyone else was even present. "What?"

"Are you sick? Don't you feel well this morning?" Mel asked, her smile fading in a kind of maternal concern she always showed the rest of the staff.

"I'm fine," he said, clearly making an effort to relax his face. "Just tired."

"Did you stay up too late last night? What were you doing?"

Jeff didn't answer Rachel's casual question. It was clear that no one suspected anything that had happened between Jeff and Vivian. They were just wondering about Jeff's strange behavior.

He wasn't as good at a game face as Vivian was.

He hadn't had nearly the practice.

"I'm just tired," he said, focusing on his coffee cup until the others realized he wasn't in the mood to talk and just left him alone.

Vivian's heart was in an uproar.

This whole situation was horrible. It wasn't just her personal pain—or Jeff's. If they couldn't get it together, then the whole staff, the whole company, would be affected by a rift between them.

She had to do something.

She had to somehow make this right.

Breakfast felt like forever, but eventually it ended. They all dispersed to return to their rooms and finish packing.

Jeff had gotten away from the others before Vivian, but she managed to catch up with him in the hallway outside their rooms.

"Jeff," she called, just before he opened his door. "Jeff, wait."

He stopped, staring at her as she hurried down the hall toward him.

"We've got to do better than this," she said, slightly breathless because the sight of him, so rumpled and serious and masculine as he stood before her, made her heart stretch in absolute yearning.

He frowned. "Better than what?"

She gestured downward to indicate the dining hall. "Better than we did over breakfast."

His frown deepened. "Better at what?"

"At pretending everything is normal. We're still business partners, Jeff. If we keep it up, we're going to destroy everything."

A flicker of grief crossed his face before it went cool again. "It's already destroyed, Vivian. I thought that was clear last night."

She gulped over the pain of those words. She wondered if he'd ever even had any doubts, or if the end of what had seemed so good between them was a simple decision for him. She managed to say, "I meant the company. I don't want to destroy that too."

It was nearly impossible for her to keep pretending that she was in control of herself, but it was felt incredibly important that she do so. She didn't want him to know how he'd crushed her.

She didn't want anyone to know.

She'd always been confident, self-sufficient.

Falling in love with Jeff shouldn't have changed that.

So she added, slightly hoarse, "That's the most important thing."

He stepped back automatically as if she had struck him, and she realized she had.

She'd just told him that the company was more important than their relationship.

Was more important than *him*.

She didn't mean it, but he wouldn't know that.

He licked his lips, his body held very still.

Then he turned away without saying a word, opened the door to his room, and stepped inside.

The door closed behind him with a soft click.

~

Vivian ended up going home with Mel.

Jeff didn't make another reappearance, and it seemed very clear that he didn't want to talk to her or be around her. She made up an excuse about Jeff needing to make a stop on the trip back home so she could have a reason for driving back with Mel rather than Jeff.

She assumed Jeff would have taken care of everything with Cecily and Balm in Gilead since he was responsible for the retreat and for the company's finances, but it felt rude to leave without saying something to Cecily, so she stopped by the other woman's office on her way to the car with her luggage.

Cecily greeted her with her typical smile—courteous, genuine, but with a controlled gentleness that seemed her approach to everyone and everything. Today she looked as prettily prim as always in a pale green sheath dress and her hair in a low bun.

"I hope you were happy with your time here," Cecily said. "I've loved having you all."

"Thank you, yes," Vivian said, fixing on a smile that she thought was probably convincing to someone who was mostly a stranger. "Everything was wonderful."

"Jeff has already taken care of everything, but is there anything else you need from me?"

"No. We're all starting to leave now. I just wanted to thank you. We might post something on our site about this place and our time here if that's okay. It will all be complimentary, of course, and it would be great exposure for you. We have a pretty big audience."

"I know you do. I follow you regularly, and I really appreciate the work you do." Cecily's eyes seemed to see more than they should. "Are you sure you had a good time here?" she asked in a different tone.

Vivian wondered what in her expression had clued Cecily in that something was wrong. "Yes. It was exactly what we were looking for here. I'm…" For no good reason her voice cracked. "I'm glad Jeff talked me into having the retreat here. You and the entire staff were wonderful. Even Zeke was really helpful, once we figured him out."

Cecily laughed. "I'm glad to hear that. Zeke is…" Something changed in her expression, as if a feeling hit her unexpectedly and altered what she was going to say. "Zeke is an acquired taste. But he's also a really good man."

"I believe it," Vivian responded. She couldn't help but think about Jeff.

Also a really good man.

And one she'd almost, almost had.

It hurt so much she couldn't breathe for a minute.

Cecily didn't say anything for a moment. Then she asked softly, "Did something happen last night?" She was a counselor by education and training, and so it was probably second nature for her to ask questions like this.

Vivian opened her mouth to deny this, to sustain her semblance that everything was normal, everything was fine.

She couldn't.

She just couldn't.

"Jeff looked like he'd been through a war when I talked to him this morning," Cecily continued. "I hadn't seen him like that all week. He'd seemed so happy. You both had."

"We were," Vivian admitted.

Cecily waited, as if checking to see if Vivian wanted to say any more. When she didn't, Cecily said, "Well, I hope you both will wait until you're home before you make any real decisions. Things don't always feel real here—since you're so cut off from your everyday world. If there's a real foundation, you built it back at home. Wait until you're home, and I think you'll see what you really want."

"I know what I want," Vivian said, speaking the absolute truth to this woman she barely knew. "But he has to want it too."

Cecily nodded, meeting her eyes with deep, clear sympathy. "Yes. That's a hard truth about relationships, and I know it better than most."

~

Vivian was afraid that Mel was going to want to talk the whole drive back to Raleigh, but the older woman was quieter than usual. It was a relief, although it left Vivian too much time to be trapped with only her own thoughts.

She was relieved when she finally got back to her own apartment, and she closed the front door behind her, feeling with strange intensity like she was finally safe, like she could finally close out the rest of the world.

She took a shower and changed into cotton pajamas. Then she turned on her television and sat down on her couch with her phone and a cashmere throw blanket.

She tried very hard to drown out all her chaotic thoughts and feelings for a few hours.

It usually worked—the kind of distraction that movies and social media provided—but it didn't work this time. She kept lowering her phone, muting the television, staring at an empty spot in the air, thinking about Jeff.

Wondering what he was doing, what he was thinking, whether he was hurting like she was.

It was getting dark when she got a Skype notification on her phone.

Seeing it was her parents, she had a brief thought that maybe she wouldn't take the call. She didn't have the will or energy to keep her game face on this evening.

And she wasn't sure she could stand anything else hurting her right now.

But she felt guilty for the idea of treating her parents like that, so she grabbed her tablet, since it had a bigger screen, and pulled up the Skype app.

Before she connected, she took a few deep breaths and tried to put on a smile.

"Hi there!" she said brightly.

Her mother was obviously about to return the greeting, but she stopped before a full word came out. "Vivian, honey, what's wrong?" she asked, her face clearly reflecting concern in the video image.

"Nothing," Vivian lied. "I'm just tired. I got back home from the retreat today, and I've already taken a shower and washed off all my makeup."

She really should have checked her face before she took this call. She'd always done so before.

"Honey, what's wrong?" her mother asked again, obviously not believing Vivian's attempt at a light excuse.

Both her parents were staring at her through the screen, their expressions sober, clearly searching her face, waiting to hear what was wrong with her.

And everything was wrong.

Everything was so incredibly wrong.

Vivian had to twist her features to hold back a wave of emotion. "It's... I don't know." Her voice broke. They would obviously know she was close to tears.

It would worry them even more.

"Tell us what happened," her mother said.

Vivian opened her mouth and tried. She really tried. But she couldn't get any words out.

"Is it something with Jeff? You seemed different about him than you ever had before, so I've been wondering about that."

"You said the other day that you'd believe I could be serious about a man when you saw it. You said I wasn't cut out for marriage." The words—the truth—closed down around her like a vise. "You were probably right."

"Well, I obviously wasn't right if it's hurting you like this. So you really love him?"

Vivian nodded, still incapable of speaking.

"And he loves you?"

"He said he did. But then he said he didn't think it was going to work." Vivian had no idea why she was admitting this. She never told anyone something so personal, so intimate.

Jeff was the only person in the world she'd ever talked to in perfect nakedness.

"And you've told him how you feel?" her mother asked, still frowning in reflective concern.

"I…" Vivian cleared her throat. "I'm supposed to tell him now, after he's broken up with me? When he's made it clear there isn't any hope?"

"It's the truth, isn't it? Why shouldn't you say it?"

Because it would humiliate her.

Because it would make her utterly helpless.

Because she just didn't do that.

Vivian sat without speaking, trying to make her mind work, trying to breathe, trying to get her throat, her chest, her whole body from hurting like this.

Her parents were obviously thinking in silence too.

No one seemed to know what to say.

Finally Vivian heard herself saying, "I feel… I feel not good enough." She had no idea how or why she was admitting that.

Her parents glanced at each other on the screen, and her mother's face twisted with emotion. "Oh, honey. Do I make you feel that way?"

Vivian tried to deny this, but holding back the tears took all her focus.

"I'm so sorry, Vivian. We never would have wanted to make you feel that way. You're so different from us—from your brother and sister. But we're so proud of you."

Then her father burst out, "We love you. We'll always love you. No matter what."

Vivian started to shake, and the tears that had been swelling in her eyes for a while now all streamed down without warning.

"Oh, honey," her mother said, her face contorting with a matching emotion. "Please don't cry. You're going to make me cry too."

Vivian grabbed a tissue and mopped up her face, trying to pull herself together so she could at least finish this conversation. "I love you both too. And it means a lot that… that you love me. But I just don't know what to do about Jeff," she said when she was able.

"That's okay. I don't think anyone really knows what to do in such situations," her mother said. "You don't have to know. You don't have to do it exactly right. You don't have to always be perfect. Just tell him the truth. Even if it doesn't fix things, at least you will have tried."

Vivian nodded, still wiping tears away.

Her mother was right. And what was more, her mother clearly cared about her and wanted to help. Both her parents did. They weren't perfect parents, but they loved her. She knew without doubt that they did.

"Okay," she managed to say. "I better do it now, or I'll never have the courage."

"Let us know how it goes," her mother said. "We'll be waiting and praying."

Vivian closed down the Skype app and sat breathing deeply for a minute. When she realized she was trying to put back on her game face, she stopped doing it and picked up the phone.

Maybe it would be better to talk to Jeff in person, but he lived a half hour away. And she wasn't sure her courage would hold out that long.

Instead, she pulled up his number and connected the call, listening to it ring, wondering what he was doing right now.

It rang so many times that she felt a drop in her stomach, thinking he wasn't even going to take her call.

She was just about to hang up when his voice was suddenly on the line. "Hello?"

"Hi," she said, her heart leaping up into her throat.

"Hi." He sounded brusque, subdued, not at all like himself.

"You... you got home all right?" It was a stupid question, but she had to say something, and she couldn't seem to blurt out the main thing, the most important thing.

"Yeah. You too, I guess."

"Yeah. Mel took me."

They were both silent for a moment.

The silence was terrible, painful, unnatural.

She couldn't let it continue—not with Jeff, who had always seemed to understand everything about her, even without her saying it.

So she blurted it out after all. "I love you."

The quality of the silence changed, but she wasn't sure exactly how.

When he didn't say anything, she said it again. "I love you, Jeff."

She heard him take a ragged breath. "Okay."

She blinked, her heart, her whole body, completely frozen. "Okay?"

"Okay."

"That's what you're saying to me?"

"I'm not sure what you expect me to say."

She made a sound she thought was impatience, frustration. But it came out as more of a sob. "I thought the problem was that I wouldn't say it."

"That wasn't the problem."

"Then what's the problem? Please, Jeff, just tell me what the problem is so I can fix it."

"The problem is you're just trying to fix it."

She was so surprised and so hurt that she literally couldn't breathe for a moment. "I don't understand," she said at last, her tone uneven, wobbly.

"The problem is you're doing what you've always done—you're trying to do the right thing, to fix the problems, to be who everyone expects you to be. And I just want to be with you for real."

"I want that too." she gasped. "I want that too!"

He paused for a several moments before he finally said, "I wish I could believe that."

"You don't believe..." She was crying again and trying to hide the sobs from her voice.

"I really wish I could," he said again, this time in almost a whisper.

She was crying so much that it was a minute before she realized he'd hung up the phone.

She sobbed for a few minutes, completely devastated by this complete rejection from the one person she'd always trusted without reservation.

When she'd managed to calm down a little, she thought about what had happened, what he'd just said.

He didn't believe her, and when she got past the pain and betrayal of the words, she started to see why that might be.

He knew her too well.

He knew how she'd always approached the world. With her game face on. Trying to ensure that she did everything perfectly, that everyone always loved her.

And now he thought she was doing the same thing with him.

He didn't know.

He just didn't know.

And she wasn't sure how to make him know that this was different, she was different, that what she wanted more than anything was to be with him for real, to go through the world with him beside her.

That she needed him—nakedly, completely, no-holds-barred.

She realized she might not be able to fix this, but she wanted him to know the truth anyway. He was as broken as she was—in different ways but in ways that made this just as hard for him as it was for her. He deserved to know the truth at least so he wouldn't think he'd thrown himself into another mistake, another woman who just didn't want him.

She thought for a long time, staring down at her phone.

Finally she got an idea.

It was a crazy idea—and not something she ever would have seriously considered if she hadn't been stretched to her breaking point.

But the more she thought about it, the more it felt like the only way to express the truth in a way Jeff might understand.

This was her, after all. Vivian Harper. The queen of fabulousness.

She glanced at herself in the mirror and saw that her face was pale and tear-streaked and completely free from makeup. She didn't look good. At all.

She wanted to reach for her purse, for her makeup— at least put a little mascara on.

She didn't though. She just opened her laptop and switched on the camera.

Then she started to talk.

TEN

Jeff didn't sleep, and he felt worse in the morning than he had the night before when Vivian's call had left him an absolute wreck.

He'd thought—vaguely hoped—that she might call back, but she hadn't, and he could hardly blame her for that.

He'd told her the truth as he understood it. But he hadn't been nice. He'd hurt her a lot, and he couldn't stand that he'd done so.

But he also didn't know what else he could do.

He went into the office early, walking into the empty office suite.

There were hundreds of unread emails in his inbox, and there was mail piled up in the box on his desk. There was a strange kind of comfort in starting to tackle it, of going through message by message, replying, deleting, filing, sorting. All of it easy, mindless, safe.

None of it would hurt him the way he was hurting now.

His office door was closed, but he was vaguely aware of other people coming in. He heard the soft buzz of their chatting outside his door.

It was Saturday, but they'd all been gone for a week. He wasn't surprised that he wasn't the only one to want to come in and catch up some this morning so it wasn't all waiting for them on Monday morning.

He'd glanced at the website and saw there was a new posting about their retreat, complete with beautiful photographs of Balm in Gilead and even some pages of the scrapbook they'd put together while they were there. It was getting tons of responses and social media shares. He wondered if Cecily was ready for the explosion of publicity this posting would be giving her and Balm in Gilead.

It hurt some. To know that Vivian had been focusing on that post last night or this morning or whenever she'd gotten it up.

She'd turned their week there into another pretty picture for the world to see.

She'd sounded so broken last night.

He'd started to wonder if maybe she'd been telling him the truth.

But she hadn't called him back. She hadn't come to see him this morning.

If she'd been real, she would have done something.

Something.

He hoped she was okay. If she was pretending everything was nice and perfect again, then she'd backslid. It just wasn't good for her.

A tap on his office door distracted him from these thoughts.

He grunted out a response, and the door opened to reveal Vivian standing in his doorway.

She looked pretty in jeans and a simple white top, her hair pulled back in a low ponytail. But she also looked exhausted, with dark shadows under her eyes.

"Can I come in?" she asked, sounding strangely hesitant.

He didn't like to hear her sound that way. It made him feel guilty—like he had treated her wrong, like he had somehow stomped out the brightness of her sweet spirit.

"Yeah," he said. When his voice was too hoarse, he straightened up and cleared his throat.

She took a few steps into his office and closed the door behind him. "Everyone came in this morning," she said, glancing behind her at the common area of the office suite. "I guess everyone had the same idea."

He nodded. He wasn't up to making small talk, although he recognized the value in trying to return to normal.

"Are you okay?" she asked in a different tone.

"Yeah. I'm not great, but I'll be okay. What about you?"

"I'll be okay too." She was searching his face strangely. "I... I posted something."

"I saw it," he said, thinking about the pretty pictures of Balm in Gilead she'd showed the world.

She stood very still, watching his face.

"What?" he asked, after a moment.

She shook off a flicker of what looked like pain. "You don't have anything to... to say about it? I didn't think it would fix things, but I thought you might..."

"I might what?" He frowned at her. "What did you think I'd have to say?"

He sounded too cool again, the way he'd sounded the day before.

Vivian's features twisted very briefly, but then she let out her breath. "Okay. I understand. I... Our time together this last week will always mean a lot to me. I hope you believe at least that."

The pain caught him off guard and stole his breath. He managed to nod. "I do."

She nodded in response. Opened her mouth as if she would speak. But then she dropped her gaze and turned around to leave his office, her face very pale.

She looked wounded.

Like he'd wounded her.

He couldn't stand the thought of it, and he had to fight the instinct to run to her, take her in his arms, make her feel better.

But he couldn't keep doing that if it was just going to hurt him in the end.

"Vivian," he said, before he knew he was going to say anything.

She turned around, her eyes wide in the way they always were when she was trying not to cry.

"I'm sorry," he said. "I really am. I told you I was in this for the long haul, but I guess I was wrong. I've... I've been hurt before."

She gave a tight little nod. "I know you have, Jeff. I know how much Kaylee hurt you. And the last thing I wanted to do was hurt you too. I do understand."

He could see that she did as she left his office. She understood and sympathized with him even though he probably didn't deserve it.

For just a moment he felt like an asshole. A selfish asshole who had run for the shore at the first sign of rough water.

Maybe that was who he was, who he'd always been at heart.

He was bothered by this thought and by the whole conversation so much he couldn't return to email. He pulled up their website and looked at the Balm in Gilead posting again, searching the captions and vaguely wondering if there was something there he needed to see.

She'd acted like it would mean something to him, but all this could do was wound him.

He looked at each picture, read each paragraph. It was beautifully done. Intelligent. Theologically insightful. Even emotionally compelling.

But it wasn't personal.

At all.

It was just her old pattern—showing that perfect, pretty face to the world.

He'd really believed they'd gotten past that, but he'd evidently been wrong.

He'd gotten to the end when he glanced at the byline and saw Grace's name there.

His mouth dropped open for a minute.

Grace had put up this post. It was done so well he'd assumed it was Vivian, but evidently not.

Grace had done this.

Not Vivian.

But Vivian had just stood there and told him she'd posted something.

He scrolled down farther on the website and saw a video post by Vivian.

This was different. He hadn't seen this.

This was what she'd been talking about.

His heart was beating like crazy as he hit Play.

Vivian's face appeared, and his chest ached at the sight of how sad and vulnerable and nervous she looked, her hair hanging messily around her face, her lips pale, her eyes red from crying.

She never filmed herself looking like this.

She never let anyone see her looking like this.

It was so surprising that it took a while for him to realize what she was even saying.

She was talking into the camera, as she sometimes did when she had something she wanted to share. But whenever she did so, she was always well prepared. She might sound casual and natural to the regular observer, but he knew she never put herself on film unless she was sure she could get it right.

She wasn't rehearsed here though. She spoke haltingly, sometimes pausing, sometimes repeating herself.

She occasionally wiped away tears as she spoke.

When he'd finally processed what was happening enough to really listen, he had to click to restart from the beginning so he wouldn't miss anything she was saying.

I know this isn't what I normally do. I'm a mess. I know. I'm not having a breakdown or anything. At least I don't think I am. I've got a broken heart, and I've been thinking a lot about what it means to be a broken person—in need of a savior. And I guess it's when our hearts are breaking the most that we see who we really are most clearly.

Jeff's mouth had fallen open as he listened to her speak, as he watched her swipe a couple of tears away as she did.

I like to make my world as beautiful as possible. You all know I do. It's what I'm good at. And I think there's something of value there. I really do. God gave us the beautiful things in this world—and our own creativity—to enjoy, to see some of his beauty in. I think it's good. But I got to the point where I tried to hide behind that, where I don't admit who I really am beneath. I have a friend. He's always telling me that I don't have to always show a pretty face to the world. I always knew he was right, but it's only now that I see how right he really was.

She was talking about him, nakedly, openly, nothing left for her to hide behind. He could barely breathe around the lump in his throat, which was pulsing with his racing heartbeat.

We're all broken in one way or another. We've all gotten our hearts broken. And no matter how much we try to pull ourselves together, to fix what's broken, to make ourselves pretty and acceptable again, we just can't do it. I can't do it. And I guess the reason I'm doing this is that I want to admit it. Be honest about who I am. I... I'm broken. And I can't fix it or make it pretty again. Only God can do that. I made a mess of a relationship that's one of the most important things in my life—and I did it because I was afraid of being vulnerable like this, of needing someone else, of showing him who I really was. But this is me. In all my brokenness. Needing him. Loving him. Even if it's never going to work out.

Jeff was almost dizzy as he tried to process what she was saying, what she obviously meant in the deepest heart of her. He couldn't believe she was putting it on camera, showing herself to the world.

For him as much as for herself.

I guess I just wanted to show my friend that all that he's invested in me over the year wasn't a waste—even if he feels like it was. She had to pause to control the sob in her voice. *So that's it. That's me. Not very fabulous when it comes right down to it. But a child of God nonetheless. He loves us when we're broken even if it feels like no one else does. He loves us because we're broken, and from that maybe we can learn to love each other too.*

The video ended there, and Jeff's eyes were burning as it concluded.

When he could focus enough to see the screen again, he saw in confusion that there weren't any likes or shares or comments on the posting.

That was strange for any posting but particularly on one like this.

He suddenly wondered if she'd set it so that only he could see it.

He wouldn't blame her.

He would never be brave enough to post something so vulnerable for the entire world to see.

He checked the settings, though, and saw that the video was public. She'd just set it to disable comments or shares.

She wasn't looking for accolades or notes of praise.

She hadn't done this as a show.

She'd done it for real.

He was almost choking on emotion as all this registered in his mind.

Then he replayed the previous conversation with Vivian.

She'd asked him if he'd seen what she'd posted, and he'd told her he had.

Then he'd dismissed it—dismissed this—as if it were nothing.

She'd thought this hadn't meant anything to him at all. That was what he'd made her believe.

And even before that, he'd made her believe she wasn't good enough, that she'd fallen short of what he'd needed in a relationship.

He'd been telling her all long that she shouldn't feel that way.

And then he'd done it to her far worse than her parents ever had.

The knowledge, the realization, the guilt washed over him in a flood, stealing his breath and freezing his muscles.

He literally couldn't move for a whole minute. Maybe longer. He lost track of time.

He jumped to his feet so quickly that his chair rolled back violently and collided with a loud bang against the file cabinet and then rolled back toward him, hitting the back of his legs.

He ignored the impact and strode out into the main room of the office.

Mel glanced up from her desk and evidently read his presence correctly. "She's already left."

Jeff swallowed over a curse and strode toward the door.

As he started down the stairs, it hit him hard that Vivian was walking home right now, thinking he didn't really love her, that she wasn't worthy of his love.

And he'd made her feel that way.

With a ragged gasp, he started to run.

He raced down the steps, nearly stumbling once and having to catch himself with the handrail. Then he burst out of the building, turned in the direction of her apartment, and sped up to a dead run.

Other people on the sidewalk turned to stare at him as he sprinted past them, but he was barely even conscious of them.

All that mattered was Vivian.

Somewhere in front of him.

Needing for him to reach her.

On the fourth block, he finally saw her golden hair ahead of him. She was walking slowly, her shoulders slumped slightly.

He kept running, and he'd built up so much momentum that he had a hard time slowing down as he reached her.

"Vivian!" he gasped, coming to a jerky halt after he'd just passed her.

She gave a little squeal of surprise at his sudden appearance. Her face was pale, and it looked like she'd been crying again. She looked confused and hurt and delicate and strong and so incredibly dear.

"Vivian," he said again, trying desperately to catch his breath so he could speak. He was panting and sweating and throbbing with heat and urgency.

She'd raised a hand to cover her mouth, obviously shocked. "What are you doing, Jeff?" she asked. "Is everything all right?" The tear tracks on her cheeks broke his heart.

He tried to speak and couldn't, so he had to raise his hand to indicate he needed her to wait a moment.

She stood perfectly still as she waited.

Passersby were slanting them very strange looks, but neither he nor Vivian seemed to care.

"I'm so sorry," he rasped, as soon as his voice worked again. "I'm so sorry, Vivian. I was the one who was wrong. I was the one who messed up. Not you. Not you."

Her face softened slightly, as if it meant something to her that he'd come after her, but she said, "It's really okay, Jeff. You were right. I was still holding back. I was still... trying not to be completely vulnerable with you. I don't blame you for not accepting that from me."

He shook his head as she started and kept shaking it as he continued, "I was more wrong than you. I was... I was judging you and making you feel unworthy, just like I've always resented your parents for doing to you. I was just scared—scared of being hurt again. I was just as scared as you were, and so I... so I was a selfish coward. I finally saw that video you posted—I hadn't seen it when we talked earlier—but you shouldn't have had to do that to reach me. I should have been here with you all along. I'm sorry, honey. You're... you're everything to me. I love you exactly as you are. And I can wait until you're ready... for saying I love you or for going public or for anything else. I promise I can wait. I'm not going to bail on you again. If you..." He paused, completely breathless and because he was suddenly terrified he'd blown his last chance with her. "If you can forgive me. If you can give me another chance."

Vivian stared at him for a few moments after he'd finished, and he could feel his racing heartbeat in his chest, in his ears, in his feet, in the air around him.

Then she gave a little sob and threw her arms around his neck.

He kind of collapsed against her as he gathered her into his arms—in absolute relief and also exhaustion.

"I love you, honey," he murmured thickly against her hair. "And I'm so sorry."

"I'm sorry too," she gasped, her arms tightening around him even more. "I love you too."

She was sobbing against him now, and Jeff felt like sobbing too. He might have messed up, but it didn't mean he had to lose everything.

She was his.

She was still his as much as he was hers.

He wasn't sure how long they hugged on the city sidewalk, but eventually Vivian pulled away from him, a rueful amusement evident beneath the joy on her face.

"You're all sweaty," she told him.

He gave a little huff of amusement. "I know. I had to run after you."

"I was just going to my apartment. You could have caught up to me there."

"I didn't want to wait that long."

She gave a little giggle, wiping the tears off her face. "I'm glad you didn't."

Jeff might have said something else. The world had turned into a blissful blur, so he wasn't really sure if he did or not. But they ended up returning to the office.

As they walked into the suite, Mel and Grace had looked up from their computer screens and Garrett and Rachel stopped talking. The others were here too. Everyone was here.

Vivian hadn't wanted to go public yet, and he was going to respect that for as long as she needed.

He took a step away from her and tried to look like everything was normal.

Vivian gave a soft laugh and reached out for him, pulling him into a no-holds-barred kiss.

There was nothing else he could do. He wrapped both his arms around her and kissed her back.

His blood throbbed in his veins with a kind of joy and knowledge and certainty he'd never felt before.

But this was right. He knew it was right.

It was real. Absolutely real, all the way down to the core.

Vivian loved him and wanted him and wasn't holding anything back. He could feel it in the way her mouth moved against his easily, he could sense it in the warm press of her body, and he knew it down to his bones.

The office erupted in cheers and claps and laughter, and it was only then that he remembered they had an audience.

He released Vivian sheepishly, keeping one arm around her, and looked around at the rest of their staff, all of whom were grinning at them.

"It's about time," Garrett said, pushing his glasses higher up his nose. "We've been waiting for you all forever."

"You have not," Vivian replied. Flushed and laughing and still clinging to Jeff's shirt with one hand. "Nothing's been happening between us before this past week."

"Oh please," Mel said with an approving smile. "It's been going on for months now. All of us have known it."

"If you say you've taken bets on when we'd get together," Jeff said with mock seriousness, "then every one of you is fired."

It turned out there hadn't been any bets.

But there had been a tally kept of all the hints and clues and loaded moments that had proved that he and Vivian were falling in love.

And then evidently all their secrecy for the past week had been completely futile. Everyone had known they'd been sneaking off together.

Looking back, he could see that his relationship with Vivian had been developing, deepening, over the past year. He'd kept pushing back the knowledge since he'd thought it was hopeless.

But the rest of the staff knew them well, and they cared about it.

It wasn't surprising they'd known all along.

~

A month later, Jeff stopped by Vivian's office to see if she was ready to head to dinner.

She was reading through a stack of papers, looking focused and serious and gorgeous in her tailored purple jacket.

"What do you have there?" he asked, frowning slightly as he tried to think through what should be on her desk this week.

"It's one of the final book proposals," she said, barely glancing up as he entered. "Garrett whittled them down to three, so you can't complain about my reading them. This one is really good."

"Which one is it?" Now that he'd discovered what she was reading and checked it off on his mind as an approved task for her to spend her time on, he was interested in her impressions.

"The one on antiques. I'm loving the sample chapter." She was clearly absorbed in it because she hadn't set the papers down or turned her attention to him yet.

He didn't really mind.

They might be together now, but she would always love and be absorbed by her work. He didn't feel like he was second place, but whatever she was doing at the moment took her full attention.

He was the same way when she walked into his office, so he could hardly complain when she did it to him.

He waited for a couple of minutes in silence until she finished the chapter and set the papers down on her desk. "This is the next book we should do for sure."

He nodded. "I thought it looked good too. We can talk to Garrett about it tomorrow."

"She even uses Isaiah 60," Vivian said with a wistful little smile. "Did you see?" There was a memory in her eyes as she met his.

He reached over to take her hand from her desk and raised it to his mouth. Pressing a little kiss on the knuckles, he murmured, "I did see that. Of course I did."

They were both remembering the exact same moment—a month ago, in that little shop on the Outer Banks, standing over an antique side table.

It was the moment when Jeff had truly believed for the first time that there might be a future for them.

A future with them together.

He was living out that future now—as miraculous as it still sometimes felt when he woke up in the morning, opened his eyes, and remembered that Vivian loved him, that she wanted him to love her.

They gazed at each other for a few more seconds until Vivian seemed to remember that she wasn't supposed to be a sappy person. With an ironic twist of a smile, she moved the book proposal back into her inbox and turned to her computer monitor.

She glanced at the new emails that had come in before she closed down the program and then shut down her computer. "You ready?" she asked, turning her head back to him as her computer screen went dark.

"Yep. I'm just sitting here waiting for you."

"Well, I'm not late. We've got more than ten minutes to walk over to the restaurant."

"Did I say you were late?"

"Your tone seemed to imply it." She was obviously not really annoyed because she slanted him an irresistible, teasing look as she got up and walked over to the mirror on the wall of her office.

He got up too and came up behind her as she was checking her hair.

"You look beautiful," he told her, speaking only the truth.

There was no other woman in the world as beautiful as she was, and nothing had ever changed this belief for him.

She rolled her eyes as she pulled the clip out of her hair and repositioned it.

"Are your parents really going to care about your hair?"

"No," she said, lowering her hands. "But I still want to look nice."

"You do look nice. I've never seen anyone who looks as nice all the time as you do." When she made another face, he added, "That's not just a delusion based on how much I love you. I mean it. You always look nice."

She was smiling as she turned around to face him, moving a little closer as she did. Her hands lifted, and she straightened his tie and collar.

"Are your parents going to care about my tie?" he asked, genuinely curious.

"No. They couldn't care less about your tie. They already love you, just from what I've told them over the past month, and I'm not sure there's anything you can do to make them love you less, unless you up and break my heart out of spite."

He moved his hands over hers and pulled them down from his tie so their hands were clasped together between their chests. "I'm not going to break your heart, Vivian. I'm going to love you forever. You know that, right?"

Her expression had been bright, clever, slightly teasing, but at his words it changed to something soft and tender. "I'm... I'm glad," she said after a long pause. "Because that's about as long as I'm going to love you."

He leaned forward to kiss her softly, but he'd learned not to let himself kiss her too deeply when they were on their way out the door.

He particularly didn't want to go to dinner with her parents—who'd just flown into town that afternoon—when he was turned on from kissing her.

When he pulled back, she lifted her hands back up to straighten his tie again.

"What are you nervous about?" he asked her, sensing something significant in the restlessness of her hands. "I thought things were going good with your parents lately."

"They are." She nodded and then lifted her eyes to meet his. "They really are."

"Then why are you nervous?"

She gave a little shrug and admitted, "I've just never really seen them without my game face before. It feels... strange."

He smiled, realizing exactly what she meant and exactly why she was feeling insecure.

It wasn't that she believed her parents wouldn't approve of him. Or wouldn't approve of her.

It was that she was trying to be genuine, real, with them—the way she was with him—and she didn't have much practice at it. It made her feel vulnerable.

He pulled her into a hug, his heart filled with so much emotion it was hard to sort out. Love and understanding and appreciation and something like pride.

That she was so amazing.

And that she was his.

"You ready?" he asked, slightly hoarse as he pulled out of the hug.

"Yes." She gave another little nod of resolution. "I'm ready. We better go, or we'll be late."

He took her hand as they left the office, waving at Mel and Hal, who were both working late this evening.

As they walked out onto the city sidewalk, he was hit with a wave of absolute contentment, leaving the work they both loved with people they loved, holding Vivian's hand.

Or almost absolute.

He'd bought an engagement ring the week before. He hadn't been able to resist it.

He just had to figure out the right time to offer it to her.

He was pretty sure she would say yes, but he didn't want to look like he was rushing her.

He just wasn't sure how much longer he could wait.

EPILOGUE

Four months later, Vivian was lying in bed, checking in on Pinterest on her phone. Grace had been responsible for the social media accounts for the past two months, and she'd gotten a lot better with writing the commentary on her pins.

In the past week, Vivian hadn't had to suggest any changes, which was a definite improvement.

Occasionally, Vivian missed doing it herself. She'd always liked social media, and Pinterest was her favorite, but it was a relief not to always feel like she had to make time to get it done.

She had plenty of other things to do, most of which she also loved.

She had a pretty amazing job, so she wasn't going to complain about not getting to do Pinterest anymore.

She adjusted in bed slightly, pulling down the little red gown she was wearing since it had gotten hiked up over her hips. She'd switched to Facebook to check things out when the door to the connecting bathroom opened and Jeff walked out.

He'd been taking a shower, and now he was wearing nothing but a towel.

The sight of his lean body distracted her briefly from her phone. He was a very good-looking man—with and without his clothes on. She had no idea how she'd missed recognizing it for so long.

He was frowning at her as he got closer to the bed. "Are you working?"

"Just looking at Facebook."

His frown deepened. "Grace is doing a great job with that."

"I know. I wasn't trying to take over. I just wanted to see what she was doing. Is that allowed?"

Jeff dropped the towel, and her eyes lowered irresistibly to what had been hidden before. "As long as you're not working in bed."

She rolled her eyes. "I'm not working in bed. Just remember this when you're doing email in bed at five o'clock in the morning."

"I only do that when you're asleep." His frown had relaxed, and he was gazing down at her with warmth, affection, and also something hotter, something that was making her pulse race. "I like to get rid of the easy stuff before I get into the office."

"I get that, but I'm not always as asleep as you believe."

"You aren't?" He crawled into bed beside her and rolled over on top of her, his body hot and heavy and hard against hers.

She twined her arms around his neck and smiled up at him. "I'm not. So I don't need to be bossed about looking at my phone in bed."

"I wasn't bossing."

"I know bossing when I hear it, and you, Mr. Owen, are sometimes rather bossy." She was still smiling, but her whole body had tightened as he rubbed himself very slightly against her.

"Okay, Mrs. Owen. I promise to work on not bossing you so much. But maybe we can get rid of the phone for the time being."

It was still amazing to her that she was actually Mrs. Vivian Harper Owen now. His wife of two weeks.

They'd only been engaged for three months, and even that had felt like too long.

But they were married now. He'd sold his big house in the suburbs and moved into her apartment with her since they had no need of a huge house yet. She couldn't remember ever being happier.

She couldn't remember ever seeing Jeff happier either. It gave her a thrill of pride and pleasure to realize she was the one who had made him so.

"Vivian?" Jeff prompted, breaking into her thoughts.

"Yes."

"Can we get rid of the phone?"

"What phone?"

He shook his head with a half smile and raised himself up enough to expose her phone, which was now resting on her belly.

He picked it up and put it on the nightstand.

"You have a thing about taking away my phone, you know," she told him, tangling her fingers into his thick hair. "You've done it many times now, going all the way back to Balm in Gilead."

"And you snuck a secret phone in back there. For Pete's sake, Viv."

She giggled fondly as she always did when he used that particular expression. She could see on his face that he enjoyed her response to it.

"Don't try to distract me," he said with a sternness that didn't make it to his eyes. "I haven't forgotten about you sneaking that phone in."

"Which you then took away from me! Just like you're doing now."

"You could stop me if you want," he said, his eyes growing hotter as he gazed down at her lying beneath him.

She gave a little sniff. "I don't really need my phone at the moment. I can think of something better to do."

"So can I." He leaned down to kiss her, smelling of soap and toothpaste and warmth and Jeff.

She loved the smell of him.

She loved everything about him.

And her body was responding already to the feeling and to his touch.

For a moment she had to wonder how she'd gone so long working side by side with Jeff and never letting him touch her this way.

He was a very good kisser. He was very good at everything. And every time it seemed to get better.

It might have taken them a long time to get together, but it was more than worth the wait.

ABOUT NOELLE ADAMS

Noelle handwrote her first romance novel in a spiral-bound notebook when she was twelve, and she hasn't stopped writing since. She has lived in eight different states and currently resides in Virginia, where she writes full time, reads any book she can get her hands on, and offers tribute to a very spoiled cocker spaniel.

She loves travel, art, history, and ice cream. After spending far too many years of her life in graduate school, she has decided to reorient her priorities and focus on writing contemporary romances. For more information, please check out her website: noelle-adams.com.

Books by Noelle Adams

Tea for Two Series
> Falling for her Brother's Best Friend
> Winning her Brother's Best Friend
> Seducing her Brother's Best Friend

Balm in Gilead Series
> Relinquish
> Surrender
> Retreat

Rothman Royals Series
> A Princess Next Door
> A Princess for a Bride
> A Princess in Waiting

Christmas with a Prince

Preston's Mill Series (co-written with Samantha Chase)
Roommating
Speed Dating
Procreating

Eden Manor Series
One Week with her Rival
One Week with her (Ex) Stepbrother
One Week with her Husband
Christmas at Eden Manor

Beaufort Brides Series
Hired Bride
Substitute Bride
Accidental Bride

Heirs of Damon Series
Seducing the Enemy
Playing the Playboy
Engaging the Boss
Stripping the Billionaire

Willow Park Series
Married for Christmas
A Baby for Easter
A Family for Christmas
Reconciled for Easter
Home for Christmas

One Night Novellas

One Night with her Best Friend
One Night in the Ice Storm
One Night with her Bodyguard
One Night with her Boss
One Night with her Roommate
One Night with the Best Man

The Protectors Series (co-written with Samantha Chase)
Duty Bound
Honor Bound
Forever Bound
Home Bound

Standalones
A Negotiated Marriage
Listed
Bittersweet
Missing
Revival
Holiday Heat
Salvation
Excavated
Overexposed
Road Tripping
Chasing Jane
Late Fall
Fooling Around
Married by Contract
Trophy Wife
Bay Song

Made in the USA
Columbia, SC
04 October 2017